Metaphorosis

September 2020

Beautifully made speculative fiction

Also from Metaphorosis

<u>Verdage</u>

Reading 5X5 x2: Duets
Score – an SFF symphony
Reading 5X5: Readers' Edition
Reading 5X5: Writers' Edition

<u>Metaphorosis Magazine</u>

Metaphorosis: Best of 20xx
Metaphorosis 20xx: The Complete Stories
annual issues, from 2016

Monthly issues

<u>Plant Based Press</u>

Best Vegan Science Fiction & Fantasy
annual issues, from 2016

from B. Morris Allen:
Susurrus
Allenthology: Volume I
Tocsin: and other stories
Start with Stones: collected stories
Metaphorosis: a collection of stories

Metaphorosis

September 2020

edited by
B. Morris Allen

ISSN: 2573-136X (online)
ISBN: 978-1-64076-177-3 (e-book)
ISBN: 978-1-64076-178-0 (paperback)

Metaphorosis
a magazine of speculative fiction
from
Metaphorosis Publishing

Neskowin

September 2020

Fetch..7
  by B. Morris Allen

Where the Old Neighbors Go....................23
  by Thomas Ha

Pages Missing From the Diary of Samuel
Pepys, Esq...63
  by David Berger

Tower of Mud and Straw I.......................99
  by Yaroslav Barsukov

Fetch

B. Morris Allen

She had died from overheating. It was an unlikely death, in the star-spark darkness beyond the atmosphere, where the outside temperature measured in single digits Kelvin. Yet temperature in space flight was a tricky thing. In Laika's case, a part of the ship had failed to separate. Torn insulation and a compromised control system had cooperated to simulate an intolerable summer day. She had died in hours.

His own cabin had multiple failsafes, multiple mechanisms to compensate for radiative heat loss, for the lack of convection, advection, conduction. And of course they watched him. Just like they'd monitored Laika, but with cameras.

He faced his favorite now, the smooth curve of glass like HAL's dark and ominous eye, but with only human intelligence behind it. "Hello," he said. It would take a year for the message to reach Earth. There was no hurry. Not anymore.

'Leica', read the white lettering curved above the purple of the lens. He'd pasted a softscreen up beside it, with a color image of Laika in her cramped training cage. She'd been unable to turn around. She'd stopped urinating.

"No need to worry, girl." After a while, he'd gotten used to the limited movement, the claustrophobia. Drugs had helped. He had his four by four by four — sixty-four glorious meters of freedom in an ungainly cube. The clumsy bulk of it didn't matter. The cube was empty of everything but air, which might as well be stored here as in the outside tanks.

He was small, of course. On the growth front, Asian and Latin genes had won out against European and Scandinavian, producing a short, blond, tan-skinned man with blue eyes. Like Laika's he liked to think; the records weren't clear, but she'd been part Husky. The New Frontiers project had loved him from the start. He could have been dreamed up in a public relations brainstorm for the brand-new United League of Earth and its shiny, attention-distracting launch to the edges of the solar system. A Swedish grandmother for robust health, a Venezuelan Wayuu one for compact durability, cancer-free grandfathers who'd survived Chernobyl and Fukushima for radiation resistance. American parents working in foreign aid who'd brought him up in Guinea, Liberia, Rwanda, Tanzania — always heading east in search of something they'd never found.

"Well, *we've* found something, haven't we, Laika?" He'd made history, in any case. Furthest man in space. First human to the Oort cloud. First to stake a claim on behalf of the United League. Even after fifty years in transit, no one had gotten here first, no one had zipped past with new technology and a shrug of apology. Earth would send congratulations, no doubt. They might even have thought to send them in advance. Despite the morning's diagnosis. Or perhaps because of it.

He'd proved it was possible, proved that with drugs and smarts and entertainment, it was possible to stay sane.

"Mostly," he acknowledged to Laika. "Mostly sane." There had been a few dark periods. Every life had those. "You helped." He reached out to stroke the screen, and she arched her neck to one side. The animation had been tricky. It had taken months to get close, years to perfect. Earth hadn't helped. Hadn't known to help, though they would have been willing.

"Cutaneous radiation injury, they said," he told Laika, though she'd heard it already. "Plus, maybe," he checked the morning's message, "leukopenia, thrombocytopenia, erythema, keratosis, and telangiectasia. But you knew that, didn't you, girl?" He'd run out of clean cloth for bandages. There wasn't enough water left to wash them effectively. He could soak them, but then the cycler took time to process the murky fluid. He'd tried boiling the ooze off the bandages in the airlock, but of course it made the water shortage worse. And then the bandages were cold. He settled for changing bandages every hour, letting the damp ones dry in the cabin until the room was oppressively dank and smelly.

"Sorry, girl," he shrugged at Laika. "Scrubber can't keep up." Only the sail controls and radio worked well these days. "Software error." He coughed, a spray of straw-pale fluid that floated across the cabin like a cloud. "Problem in the flesh drive." Laika cocked her head and wagged her tail to laugh.

Would he have lived longer on Earth? It seemed unlikely. Less radiation, of course. If he'd avoided Luanda, Bishkck, Winnipeg, and the other places the UL had pacified. Had there been more, after he left? It didn't matter. New Frontiers had taken him on, more sold on his heritage than on hard-won but second-rate degrees in astronomy and medicine, but they'd taken him. He owed them for that, anyway.

And for Mor-Mor. After the terror attacks, she'd been the only family he had left. A bedridden old Swedish woman in a flat in a suburb of Vänersborg, itself now a suburb of Trollhättan. She'd lived only for weekly visits from the therapy dogs, and video-chats from one lone grandson, when he could afford them.

"She didn't have you though, did she, girl?" Laika wagged and barked. "That's the spirit." Mor-Mor had believed firmly in spirits — and ley-lines and charms and all the things her Methodist parents had disapproved of. 'Your parents' spirits are somewhere in the world,' she'd told him. 'It's just up to you to find them.' But when his search had taken him off Earth, she hadn't fought it.

'I need to go,' he'd told her. And, because he wanted to do it, really wanted to, and because he had nothing else, she'd let him go. 'Take this,' was the only thing she'd said, and sent a scan of Laika, faded black and white from some old newspaper, stained with the tears she'd wept back in the 20th century, and in the years since. 'I want to go,' he'd assured her, though she already knew. 'I choose to go.'

He wouldn't trade it for anything, half a century on. He'd accomplished little beyond a study in isolation, little that an automated probe could not have done better. He'd read up on the law, during his voyage, confirmed that the trip was more symbolic than precedential, and let it go. He'd read thousands of books, written a handful of his own.

"I had to go," he told Laika now. The pay for his effort had settled Mor-Mor in an elegant home with a view of the dog park, bought her the best care that he'd never told her was his real reason for going. The rest had funded a small dog rescue foundation. Would he have accomplished more had he stayed, worked his way out of poverty and into the middle class like a few lucky others? In her last message, some forty years back, now, she'd told him he was right to go. It was hard to tell, through the UL censors, but he'd taken it as a confirmation that things had gotten worse. He'd sent her back a still from his Laika simulator, then capable of little more than an exaggerated doggy grin.

"But you can do more than that now, can't you girl?" She wriggled and rolled over in her little space. It took some maneuvering. "Of course you can."

He'd done some wriggling himself, over the years. When even the drugs weren't enough to calm him, when he needed motion, he had the Track — a circular tube running around the outside of his cube. A meter wide; just enough to pull himself along in endless circles, or to pump his legs a bit on the clever ratchet-cycle New Frontiers had built.

There was more room now, of course. On two ends of the cube, a hatch led to empty tanks and holds. If he wanted, he could pressurize them, wander past their complex struts and bulkheads like a spelunker exploring lost caverns.

"After a while, the space doesn't matter," he told Laika. "Your perspective shifts." All that food and water had provided shielding. Laika had had none, but she hadn't lived long enough for it to matter. Here, the cycler reused everything it could. Over a fifty-year journey, though, there were losses. The holds were bare now. Over the years, they'd held spares, gardens, waste, play areas, meditation chambers. There had been years when he lived in them, heedless of exposure. Years when he'd hidden in his little cube core. Now it made no difference. He checked his bandages, an old jumpsuit torn in strips. The seepage wasn't bad. Not troubling.

"Is it time?" he asked Laika. She quirked her head to one side, ears cocked. "Do you think it's finally time?" She quirked her head the other way, eyes eager, tongue lolling just to the edge of her teeth. "It's now or never, girl." They'd given him a year to live, the UL doctors, in the message they'd sent a year ago. "Shall we do it?"

"Arf!" she replied, with a naughty gleam in her eye.

"I thought so too," he agreed. And of course he'd been planning this for years. Ever since Mor-Mor died, in a way.

"I'm turning the sail," he announced to his distant audience. They still listened, still watched. He got weekly messages, advice on problems no longer relevant, suggestions for synthesizing drugs from materials long out of inventory, advice on how to compact waste he'd long since dumped. "I'll be out of touch for a while." It was a dereliction of duty, his first in fifty conscientious years. Without the sail to focus their faint signals, he would no longer hear Earth's messages, no longer be able to send his own.

"We did our part, though, didn't we, girl?" Laika grinned back. "I think we did." With a twinge of guilt and uncertainty, ruthlessly suppressed, he tapped the icon for his pre-calculated sail shift. It would take weeks.

He set the second program running. He'd recorded his message over months, short as it was. "I wanted to get it just right," he told Laika and the lens that no longer transmitted his image and voice. In the circuits behind the control panel, gates opened and closed, feeding a short, recorded message to the radio in a cycle of thousands of slightly different iterations. "It was mostly programming and calculation, actually." He scratched her head, and she bowed her neck in pleasure. Her tail thumped against her cage, only the tip visible beyond the curve of its metal roof.

"I'll just check the readouts," he said, withdrawing his hand.

"Arf!" she said, asking for more scratching. When none came, she lay her head down between her paws and settled into her resting state. This far from the Sun, energy was scarce. The micro-reactor worked only at a low level, and battery capacity had dwindled with time.

The sailcord readouts were tied to the main screen, of course, but he liked to climb out and check the physical gauges when he could. He still had a working pressure suit, and of course exposure didn't matter anymore. He tied another layer of cloth around his weeping chest. Body fluids loose in the suit could get in the circuits if they really tried. More important, they smelled bad. He smelled bad enough already. He felt bad for Laika, with her more sensitive nose. Of course, she was just a simulation.

Out on the hull, the sail was responding just as his simulation had predicted. It was early to say much, of course. The frozen bearings on #27 and the broken tension-pulley on #41 had required a little workaround, but it seemed to work just as it should.

He floated for a while sun-side. It didn't matter anymore if he drifted a bit. In the early days, the focus of the sail had been a dangerous place to be; it would have burned through his suit in seconds. Now it was barely warm.

Thousands of AUs away, Sol was a small, bright dot. "Bye," he said, and waved, as if he hadn't said his farewells years before. The motion set him slowly spinning. The view didn't change much. At this distance, even Sol didn't look like much. He watched as the Milky Way slowly circled around him until the tension in his twisting safe-line stopped him and set him spinning back the other way. "Hi."

They'd tried to stop him, of course, the do-gooders and the Luddites and the religionists. 'It's not fair,' they'd said, and 'You'll draw the attention of aliens,' and 'Man was meant to live on Earth.' But he'd had no family, and he'd been young and handsome, and he'd had the League behind him, and the scientists, and the fear that the Confederation might get there first.

"Looks like we're out here alone," he told Laika. "No aliens. No angels. Darn." He tugged the safeline to set him moving slowly back to the ship. "And this way, I got to be with you." Mor-Mor had cried the day he left. 'Go find her,' she'd said. "And I will," he said now. "I know you're out here somewhere, kid." Because where else could the soul of a spacedog go? "Playing with those aliens, probably, eh?"

Somewhere in the ship, an algorithm parsed the statement, generated a response. "Arf!"

Back inside the ship, he listened to the messages that still accumulated despite the slowly-turning sail. Long-winded bureaucrats celebrating last year's 49th anniversary. Curt doctors detailing treatments he'd long since tried. Dull chemists proposing supplements scraped from hull surfaces and worn out suit parts.

He listened to it all. "Never know, eh girl? Might be something good in there." After a few days, the sail had shifted enough that the messages were too broken for the computer to reconstruct. "Now we're really alone, hmm?" He checked the telltales. His message continued to go out in different codings, on different frequencies, as the sail slowly turned.

He slept for a time, woke with a start. "Thought I heard you barking." He stroked her neck. "Not you, hmm?" She reached out a paw for more scratching, and he rubbed a hand on each side of her neck, setting her wriggling like a puppy in her restraints. "Not yet. Not long."

He had no energy now to eat, and the water from the cycler was cloudy. "Smells bad, too. Well," he coughed, and droplets of red floated up to dot the camera lens. "You did without water. Guess I can too." He turned the speakers on so that he could hear his message, still transmitting, still repeating.

He settled his head comfortably against a cushion on the bulkhead, and listened to Laika breathing softly in his ear. Her muzzle came down soft against his shoulder and he smiled. "Good night, girl," he murmured. As his eyes grew dull, she settled into rest mode.

In the still of the cabin, a recording played on. A whistle, high, then low. Then an enthusiastic call, "Лайка, вернись домой. Тебе пора отдыхать." *Laika, come home. It's time to rest.* At the outer hatch, a scratching sound might have been the scrabbling of claws, asking to come in.

See B. Morris Allen's story "Fetch" online at Metaphorosis.
If you liked it, leave a comment. Authors love that!
Remember to subscribe to our e-mail updates so you'll know when new stories are posted.

About the story

In 1957, the USSR sent a dog on the second craft ever to enter Earth orbit, Sputnik 2. The ship was never intended to be recovered, but Laika, a part-Husky street dog, died within hours of takeoff. When Adilya Kotovskaya settled Laika into her cramped space on Sputnik, she said "Please forgive us." Oleg Gazenko, who chose and trained Laika, later said, "The more time passes, the more I'm sorry about it. We shouldn't have done it. We did not learn enough from the mission to justify the death of the dog."

We've done a lot of terrible things to animals in the name of science (and continue to do them). The cruelty of Laika's death has haunted me since I was a child. My favorite film is Lasse Hallstrom's *My Life as a Dog*, in which a boy ponders what was done to Laika. This particular story, though, was inspired by a song from Tony Carey's Planet P Project, "Saw a Satellite", which includes the lines, "And the ratings went over the moon on the day Laika died / But my mother just stayed in her room all morning and she cried". I wanted to write something that both recognized the evil we did to Laika, but had a more hopeful, optimistic tone. I'm not sure it worked on the optimism front, but despite its grim inception, the story is intended as a positive message about coming to terms with the errors of the past.

Where the Old Neighbors Go

Thomas Ha

The man standing on the porch that night seemed like an ordinary gentrifier at first glance: young and tall and artfully unshaven. His jeans were tattered, but strangely crisp, and his shirt was loose and tight in all the wrong places. He had the appearance of someone vaguely famous, like his face could have been in a magazine ad or on the side of a bus. And to anyone other than Mary Walker, he would have successfully passed for a human.

Mary widened the opening of her front door, knowing she could no longer avoid him. She clutched the edges of her stained bathrobe and stared up at the man through the tangle of her grey and white hair.

He smiled, and there was something off, as if his features were meant to be stationary, not stretched in that way. "I thought I should finally introduce myself," he said. "I'm the new neighbor."

The man gestured over his shoulder toward the house across the street. It was an ashen block of concrete and glass, with sharp and modern angles, sitting on a pristine lot with a newly paved driveway. Every time Mary looked at it, she felt nauseous.

"I was wondering what you'd be like," she said.

"And?"

"I don't see any horns," Mary replied.

He laughed, and it, like his smile, seemed out of place. "I was wondering if we could talk, get to know one another. Unless this is a bad time?"

Mary pushed her hair from her eyes and looked out at the dark street. No dog-walkers or joggers in sight. "Why don't you come in?" she said, standing aside.

The man was already through the entryway before she had finished her sentence, peering at Mary's walls and looking around the corner into the den. "What a lovely home," he said monotonously.

Mary tightened the frayed belt of her robe and walked behind him, watching as he ran his fingers along one of her sideboards and around the rim of a decorative vase. He paused at the sectional sofa in the center of the living room, then looked to Mary, as if inviting her to sit.

Mary needed no invitation in her own home. She went to an orange armchair in the corner and dropped into it comfortably, then pointed a bony finger at the sofa. The man sat at her direction, a glimmer of annoyance in his eyes.

"So," Mary began. "You're the one who bought Frank Abra's home."

He nodded. "I met him very briefly after the closing. Nice guy."

"Hm." Mary rested a weathered cheek on her hand. "A lot of people on the hill have been selling lately. But Frank? Didn't strike me as the type."

"Truth be told, I don't know much about him," he shrugged. "I think the house was getting to be too much to maintain." The man glanced at other rooms that were visible from where he sat. "You live alone too, don't you?"

Mary ignored the question. "Frank was getting on in years," she said, scratching at a mole next to her eye with her index finger. "Still, I was surprised—not so much as a for-sale sign, let alone a goodbye. First time I knew what happened was when you got rid of the house."

She vividly remembered the day Frank's place had been demolished last spring.

It had started with a rumbling that made her get out of bed and look out the front window. Mary had watched as a slow-moving caravan of construction vehicles proceeded down the road, then encircled the small, Craftsman bungalow across the street.

She had emerged from her home in her bathrobe and marched over the low bushes in her front yard, waving a hand at one of the drivers.

"Hey!" she yelled. "What're you doing?"

"What's it look like?"

"Where's Frank?" She shaded her eyes with one hand and looked up.

"Ma'am, I don't know who Frank is, but he isn't here. You better back up!"

The construction vehicles roared to life, and the ground began to vibrate as they inched across the lawn.

One of the bulldozers began by tearing through the planks of the front deck. It was an uncovered porch that Frank had built with his wife, Callie, in the Sixties. He hadn't had the strength to repair it in over a decade, so the wood splintered and folded like toothpicks as the bulldozer's blade rippled through with no resistance.

An excavator then approached the side of the house and raised its boom, reminding Mary of an animal rearing to strike. The bucket came down and clawed open a hole in one of the walls, bricks raining down onto the dirt. Mary could see into the home through the wound, the lilac-patterned wallpaper in one of Frank's bedrooms shredded. Several minutes later, the wall next to it, adjacent to Frank's chimney, came apart like cardboard.

Mary covered her nose and mouth with her hand, watching as the sections of Frank's house came undone. Even after the machines left, she lingered on the street and walked through the lot where Frank's home had been, a pile of dirt and rubble that was peppered with pieces of what used to hold the house together.

Mary returned her attention to the young man now sitting on her sofa, trying her best to push the image of the ruined Abra home from her mind.

"Did Frank mention where he was headed?" she asked.

"You know," the man furrowed his brow, "I don't think he did. But I'm sure I have his agent's number somewhere if you'd like to get in touch."

"That's nice of you to offer." Mary leaned on the other side of the armchair. "But enough about Frank. What about you? What brings you to the hill?"

The young man stretched his arms over the back of the sofa, making it a point to show how comfortable he was. "I just really like the neighborhood," he said. "Quiet and removed. There's a good energy about it. And the people seem nice."

"Do they?"

"Relaxed, I guess."

"Relaxed," Mary repeated. "I suppose that's one way to put it."

Mary would have described her neighbors as oblivious.

Not one of them had seemed concerned about Frank when he disappeared. For days after his house was demolished, Mary had gone door to door to see if anyone had heard where Frank was, or even that he was planning to leave.

None of the neighbors had answers, let alone cared.

Of course, it might have had something to do with who was asking. Several of them slammed their doors in Mary's face at the sight of her. Others simply pretended they weren't home. Mary could feel their eyes trailing her from their windows, and a few of them who had known Mary from better days, before she had become this way, had a certain look on their faces that she absolutely could not stand, as if they pitied her.

"Are you...taking care of yourself, Mary?" One of the older neighbors looked down at her bathrobe with concern.

"What's to take care of?" Mary scoffed. "It's not like I'm having company anytime soon, am I?" She pushed the tangled strands of her hair out of her face. "I'm just comfortable as I am, thank you very much. But about Frank—"

"I'm sorry, but I really don't know," they said. "You please take care, though, okay, Mary?" The door shut slowly, and Mary muttered to herself as she moved on. She made doubly sure to meet every gaze as she marched down the street, before they each turned away, one by one.

One of the neighbors she did manage to catch at the door, a middle-aged man who lived a few houses down the block, listened to her just long enough to hear her mention Frank's name before interrupting.

"If I tell you what I know," he said, "will you stop calling parking enforcement and asking them to tow my goddamn car?"

Mary was used to these confrontations, and she knew that if she wasn't firm about the way things ought to be, the others would walk all over her. Still, she preferred the honesty of this over the feigned sympathy she got from the others.

"If it doesn't have a permit on the dash, I have to call," she replied. "Could belong to some prowler."

"It's *my* car! You *know* that!"

"I really don't like to assume, you know? Anyway, listen, about Frank—"

This door, like all the others, shut on her.

Mary grimaced to herself as she remembered, but paid it no mind. In her several decades of living on the hill, her neighbors had never understood how her watchful eye kept danger away from their homes. But she didn't need their approval to keep things in order.

The young man on the sofa cleared his throat, trying to draw her back into the conversation. "If it's not too much trouble, could I maybe get something to drink?"

"Ah." Mary sat up straight and then pulled herself out of the armchair. "Of course. I've already forgotten basic hospitality. What would you like?"

"Water would be fine."

"Coffee," she said to herself. "It's late, but I think I'll need it for a chat like this. Would you like a cup?"

"Well, actually I said—" the man shifted, seemingly unsure if she was hard of hearing. "Sure. Coffee is fine."

Mary shuffled to the other side of the den, leading the young man, who followed close behind her, through a dining room and into a kitchen in the northwest corner of the house. It was brightly lit, with soothing blue walls and shining tile that Mary scrubbed daily. She pointed absentmindedly to a breakfast nook in the corner, and the young man went over and sat in a chair.

Mary let her fingers run across the marble countertop as she moved around the kitchen in a practiced manner. She took two cups from her favorite, but rarely used, china set, gently placing each one next to the sink before producing a pour-over glass coffee maker from another cupboard and eyeing the curved, transparent body under the light just to make sure that there were no unsightly water marks. She brought out a tin filled with ground coffee she'd harvested from the cherries in the backyard, the earthy, gritty smell soothing her while she continued to assemble what she needed.

As she gathered the accoutrements, her mind began to drift, recalling other times when she used to make things in the kitchen for more than just herself, when the thudding of little feet and high-pitched giggling echoed through the halls, joining the sounds of the sink-water rushing and glasses clattering as she stood at the countertop.

But then Mary remembered where she was again, and more importantly, whom she was with, and the pleasantness vanished.

"Hospitality is important, you know," Mary said, more to herself than the man sitting at the nook, as she focused herself again and removed a coffee filter from the bottom of a small box. "Across all cultures, the code between guest and host is paramount. The Greeks had a special word for it…"

"Xenia," the young man replied.

"Xenia," Mary nodded, pouring the ground coffee on top of a filter and setting a kettle to boil. "That's right. So you're familiar. You have to be at your best, because you never know who, or what, could be visiting you."

"I like that." The young man leaned back, watching Mary carefully as she stood at the kettle.

"In the old stories, some of the worst monsters were the ones who broke that code. Innkeepers that preyed on guests. Bandits who took advantage of generous hosts. It takes something particularly nasty to do that in a home. Homes are sacred."

The water came to a boil.

Mary grabbed the kettle and poured the water over the coffee pot, and the hot liquid dripped down into the glass body, filling it gradually. "Milk? Sugar?"

"Black is fine."

"Black it is." She poured the two cups and brought them over.

The man took the steaming cup and raised it to his lips, blowing gently and about to drink, when he noticed that Mary was watching him. Something about the coffee smelled unusual and caused him to stop.

He laughed, but in a way that seemed genuine for the first time that night—an angry cackle mixed with shock.

Mary drank from her cup and looked back at him. "What is it?"

She knew he had detected it.

Mary always mixed small pieces of aspen bark into her coffee, so that its flavor would seep into the drink. Its effect on ordinary people was negligible, but on things like Mary's visitor, it could have irreparable consequences.

"So much for xenia," he said, staring intently at the dark, rippling fluid in the cup in front of him.

"Had to try," Mary shrugged.

In truth, she knew this visit had been coming for some time. She had lived too long, and too cautiously, to ignore the warning signs.

After she couldn't turn up any information on Frank, she had gone, as she often did, to her other sources.

Mary set out early one morning up a dirt path behind her house toward the peak of the hill that overlooked the neighborhood. There was a wooded area, filled with blackened trees that had been caught in a brushfire long ago, yet never managed to die or sprout new growth. She followed the path for a few minutes before turning off from it, keeping track of small knife marks she had left in certain trunks.

Finally, at the heart of the woods, she found the carob tree, grey and knotted. She came within ten feet of it and stopped.

"I need to talk," she said.

The leaves rustled, and there was grunting from some unseen space within the branches. The shaking subsided, and there was a silence before something emerged.

Yellow Eyes peeked his head out, appearing in the form of a large, black crow with greasy feathers.

"Whatever it is, I didn't do it," he said. "Haven't been near any of the folks, just like we agreed." The bird shuffled along the branch and turned its head, the ring of one of its eyes focused on her.

Mary watched Yellow Eyes closely. There were times when he would start a conversation, then pounce on her without warning. The last time he had done that, he had been wearing the body of a copperhead, and she could not feel her hand for over a year after.

"Spoken like an innocent," Mary said. "But no. Someone new is moving to the neighborhood and seems like your type."

"My type?" Yellow Eyes said. "You'll have to be more specific. Charming? Good conversationalist?"

Mary turned around and began to walk away.

"Wait." Yellow Eyes fluttered down from the branch and to the ground in front of the woman. "I'll tell you anything you want, if you just, you know…"

The bird gestured with his head toward the circle of pale, purple petals around the carob tree, sprouting up from under the grass and weeds on the forest floor, ever-blooming and just as vibrant as they had been when Mary planted them years ago.

Mary had learned at a young age that creatures like Yellow Eyes could never be confronted directly. Instead, there were other ways, mostly forgotten but still passed down in some families, or buried in books, which Mary made some effort to collect over the years. With the right tools and enough time, she knew she could hold her own against them.

In the case of Yellow Eyes, it took patience, but Mary had meticulously tracked him to his nest after he'd first chosen the crow body. She waited until he was away to seed the circle of vervain, then waited months more as the circle strengthened beneath him and bloomed.

This particular seal, the traveler's knot, was one of the better ones she had crafted in her time on the hill. The living pattern of vervain connected him, not just to the mortal form of the bird he had chosen, but to the tree he had made his home. If anything happened to either the crow or the carob, Yellow Eyes would feel every bit of it, and if the damage was great enough, there were no new bodies that could save him from death. It was a terrifying prospect for a creature who was supposed to live forever.

"Tell me what you know, and I'll decide if it's worth your release," Mary said.

Yellow Eyes crept closer, cocking his head one way and then the other. He drew his beak wide and exposed a row of round, human-like teeth, grinning. "I might have heard about someone who's headed this way. But this one, if it is who I think it is, is definitely not my 'type'."

"Meaning what?"

"Meaning, you know me," Yellow Eyes said. "I'm old-fashioned. I like tricks and deals, the art of a good bargain. But these new things that are coming up now—they're emptier and hungrier, no patience for the craft. They don't get any enjoyment out of the chase the way some of us do."

"Then what do they want?"

"What does any monstrous little toddler want? They want to take everything you have, just as soon as they can swallow it."

Yellow Eyes drew closer to Mary. He puffed his chest and spread his clawed feet on the ground, exposing another set of long, dark fingers between his thin crow toes that curled into the dirt.

His tongue flopped out of his mouth as he salivated, growing overexcited.

Mary could see that Yellow Eyes was beginning to forget himself. She moved slowly to the trunk of the carob tree and reached a hand to the lowest branch, thin enough that she could bend it, but substantial enough that it would work for her.

She snapped it.

Yellow Eyes shrieked as the traveler's knot connected him to the sensation of the branch breaking. He dropped to the ground and twisted in pain as if one of his bones had cracked.

"Settle down," Mary said sharply.

Yellow Eyes shrank and gave the closest thing a bird could to a grimace as he breathed through the pain. "Listen," he heaved, "A couple of little Mary Walker tricks aren't going to cut it with this one. He'll break you in half before you can get anything past him."

"Hm," Mary replied, wondering what she would do if that were true. She knew she would have to think this through carefully in advance.

"So?" Yellow Eyes turned his head, wincing. "You asked; I answered. That clears our ledger, I think."

"Does it?" Mary stared down at the creature. "All I learned was that this stranger is tougher than you are, which," she waved at the vervain flowers, "doesn't tell me much at all."

"Oh, come on." Yellow Eyes flapped his wings. "I played nice, and you can't keep me under the power of this seal forever."

"If I survive, I'll give it some thought." Mary headed back toward the dirt path.

"Mary. Are you serious?"

She waved and kept walking.

"This is why no one likes you," Yellow Eyes screeched. "Mary!"

His cawing carried over the hill, and she heard him for most of the walk back through the woods.

But it turned out, in the end, that Yellow Eyes had been right about Mary's visitor.

The young man didn't seem interested in engaging with, outwitting, or deceiving her. He looked down at the cup of coffee in front of him, dosed with aspen, and his resting expression shifted, almost imperceptibly.

His eyes moved very deliberately from the cup in his hands, up to meet Mary's face.

"I prefer it this way," he said. "Really."

Mary began to retort as she stood up from the nook, but the man interrupted her.

"*Sit,*" he said quietly.

The old woman felt her body fold into the seat, like a hand had gripped the back of her neck and pushed her firmly into place, forcing her to stare at the man across from her.

"A little bird told me you were going to be trouble," he said.

Mary's brow creased at the mention of Yellow Eyes, but she did her best to keep her expression neutral. It seemed Mary's visitor had more information about her than she anticipated and, like her, had prepared himself in advance of this night.

The young man pushed his cup across the table. "You know, the thing I enjoy most about a fresh brew is the aroma, flavor...and heat. *Pick it up.*"

Mary's hand moved of its own accord, taking his cup and bringing it closer.

"*Pour it on your hand. Slowly.*"

It had been a long time since Mary had met someone with a silver tongue as strong as his. There were ways to fight this kind of persuasion, with enough preparation and the right tonics, but she knew that it was futile now to try.

She tipped the cup and watched as the steaming liquid spilled onto the back of her other hand, which was firmly pressed on the surface of the table. Little splatters of coffee bounced off of her skin as her hand grew patchy, red and white blisters beginning to form. Mary did her best not to react, but her breathing grew faster and shallower as her eyes watered. She bit deep into her bottom lip as she felt the pain searing up through her arm.

Rivers of coffee joined around her hand and cascaded off the edge of the table, splashing to the tile below.

"Does it hurt?" the young man asked. "It's hard to tell with you."

Even though she could not stop it, Mary wasn't powerless. There were methods she had learned, still taught by older members of certain monasteries who were wary of creatures like this, that were used to slow the connection from the nerves to the mind, even if only for a few seconds.

Mary breathed steadily and concentrated on the sharp, vibrant smell of the coffee, recalling the way it often drifted up the stairs and along the corridors of the house, up to the bedroom on the second floor, and how, when it did, she could pick up its bitter fragrance, even when she was wrapped in layers of her thick, down blankets early in the morning. She was transported to those chilly hours after sunrise when someone else was brewing a pot, and she could hear the whistling of the kettle as she kept her eyes closed, still fading in and out of consciousness. She recalled her daughter's footsteps, her tiny hands pressing Mary's cheeks and poking her nose while Mary pretended to sleep for a little bit longer.

Mama?

Mary trembled until the last drop of coffee had run out, but she did not make a sound.

When she opened her eyes, the young man seemed to be watching her intently, masking just a hint of frustration. His gaze turned to the second cup of coffee, still steaming, but before he could speak, Mary knocked the cup with the back of her red, blistered hand. It flew off the table and shattered on the kitchen floor with a burst that soaked the floor.

The man crossed his arms. "Now why would you do that? I could just make you refill your cup from the pot, you know."

Mary gripped her burned hand and stared silently.

The man moved over in his chair to a spot at the table that wasn't dripping with coffee. He rested his elbows on its surface and put his chin on his clasped hands. "Go on," he said softly. "Cool that hand. And while you're at it, clean this up."

Mary went to the sink and ran her hand under the cold water. She grabbed a wet cloth from a rack and wrapped her fingers, then took another rag to wipe up the coffee.

"I really meant it earlier, you know," the young man said as he watched her clean the floor. "This is a lovely home. Nicer than I would have expected from the way you keep yourself."

"Thanks," Mary replied dryly, throwing the fragments of the cup in the trash and wringing the rag out in the sink.

"It's obvious you have a real reverence for all these *things*," he waved at the furniture and the decorations surrounding him. "You've practically built a museum here, of fonder times perhaps?" The man gave a knowing half-smile and picked up the other cup on the table, holding it to the light and peering at the sides and the bottom. "But no matter how much meaning and memory you imbue these things with, they'll eventually fall apart. Just like you."

He let the cup drop from his hand and crash to the tile floor below, its pieces scattering in every direction.

"Prick," Mary muttered, getting back on the floor.

"What was that?"

She huffed as she stood, then wiped the table in the breakfast nook before throwing the last few shards away. "You heard it."

"You know." He sat forward. "I could burn this place to the ground, with you still in it. And I wouldn't even have to blink."

"Not likely," Mary replied.

"What?"

"Not likely," she repeated. "If that were true, you'd have done it. You wouldn't waste your time with this coffee and small talk," Mary said. "It's clear you want something from me, or I'd be dead."

His eyes darkened. "Maybe this is it. Maybe I want you to suffer."

"Not likely."

"Stop saying that."

"You would have picked a budding young woman to torture or a family to harass. But an old lady like me has no value, and no value, no entertainment."

The young man tapped the table with his fingers.

"We both want this over with, don't we?" she asked. "What's the point in dragging it out now?"

The man appeared loath to admit it, but Mary could tell that he was growing impatient. After a minute of silence, he reached into his jeans pocket and pulled out a piece of paper, unfolded it and put it down for Mary to see.

She picked it up and read it over as she sat down across from him again. "A quitclaim?" she muttered. Mary studied the language of the document a second time. It was a run-of-the-mill human deed for her property, as far as she could tell. Mary had seen a lot of gambits by his kind, but never anything so pedestrian.

"What could someone like you want with my land?" she asked.

"Doesn't matter." The young man's face went purposefully blank. "But the fact that this also gets you out of this neighborhood now strikes me as a bonus."

Mary ignored the insult and read the document again, trying to guess at what the man was leaving unsaid. She assumed that if he could have forced her to sign, he would have already, but something prevented it. He could try to charm, frighten, or bully her, but, in the end, he wanted this transfer to be voluntary for some reason.

"What about the formalities?" Mary asked. "Price, notarization, things like that?"

"The price is whatever you tell me it is. The rest I can make happen tonight, once you sign. It's just paper, after all."

"And is this the deal you made with Frank Abra?" she asked.

The young man stared back without answering.

Of course, Mary already knew what had happened to Frank without the man saying anything. Weeks after the Abra house was demolished, Mary had visited the lot across the street after sundown, when the construction workers were gone.

She had seen that most of the rubble had been dumped, and a giant pit was ready to be filled with concrete for the house's foundation. Mary brought an old metal detector she had gotten at a garage sale years earlier, barely used except for clearing out rusty nails and other debris in her garden. She paced across the Abra lot, waving the detector around, mostly finding coins and scrap, until she eventually came across a piece of jewelry a few feet from where the new house was to be built.

She reached down and pulled a window locket from the soil.

Mary wiped it with the sleeve of her bathrobe and inspected it. She remembered seeing Callie Abra wear the locket every day as she stood out on the lawn and watered their garden, and, after she passed away, Mary saw Frank put it around his neck too, never once putting it aside or taking it off, always grasping it like it was the most important thing on earth. The fact that it was here, and he wasn't, told her everything she needed to know.

Mary slid it into the pocket of her bathrobe and looked around at the lot one more time.

The truth was that she and the Abras had never really been that close. On the best days, she was polite with them, and on the worst, the whole street could hear their screaming matches.

And yet, Mary realized, as she knelt in the dirt, that the neighborhood felt quieter and lonelier without them.

Her fingers crept to the ground, and she touched the soil, feeling its dampness.

Mary remembered the soil as she stared at the young man in her kitchen, thinking of what best to say.

"What will happen to the neighborhood?" she asked him.

"What?"

"The hill. What will you do to them?"

The man shifted in his seat and squinted at her, as if puzzled by her question. "You know, when I first moved here and asked around, it was funny. I didn't even have to pry. Yours was the name that almost inevitably came up when people talked about this street."

"Guess I'm popular," Mary replied flatly.

"Lady Bathrobe," he said. "The Hag on the Hill. Old Tangle-Hair. The Parking Permit Crusader. The Groaning Crone."

"A couple of those are clever, but the rest are objectively bad."

" 'Nobody cares about her,' 'Lives alone for a reason,' they told me." The young man watched Mary sink visibly in her chair. " 'Why doesn't she do everyone a favor and just die?' "

Mary squeezed her burned hand.

"They don't even want to look at you. Just the sight of your filthy robe and ratty hair puts them on edge. Most of them wish you would just disappear and never come back." He shook his head. "I know I'm not telling you anything you don't already know."

"So what?" she said softly.

"So, why do you care what happens to this place after you leave?" The man pushed the deed closer to Mary. "You don't need this hill, and if I've learned anything, it's that the hill *certainly* doesn't need you."

Mary lowered her chin and reached into the pocket of her bathrobe. She felt for the Abras' locket, which she kept there now out of habit, and she touched its smooth, metal edges. For the first time, she didn't have a pithy response for the young man, and he seemed pleased.

"How about, instead of pouring your energy into this house and this hill, maybe you take care of yourself, for once, and enjoy those golden years?" He pinched the sleeve of her tattered bathrobe and smirked. "Because whatever it is you're trying to preserve, it's gone, lady. You've got to see that."

The young man seemed like he was finished speaking and sat back down. Nothing about what the man said changed what Mary was going to do next; in truth, she had made that decision some time ago. But still, when it was quiet again, Mary realized she felt a chill, one that usually visited her when she couldn't fall asleep, and it touched her more deeply than anything else that had happened that night.

After a few seconds, Mary stood and began to walk from the kitchen. The young man followed her, through the study and dining room, and back to the den. Mary approached one of the windows at the front of the house and moved back a heavy curtain, so that she could see across the street clearly.

"There." She pointed at his home, the block of concrete and glass, its modern architecture and chic exterior, like a blight on the hill.

"What about it?"

"You want me to sign? Then I want something first. Whether I leave or not, I can't stand the idea of that shitbox sitting there instead of Frank's place. Makes me sick." Mary gestured over her shoulder. "So let's see if you were telling the truth. Burn it to the ground without blinking, or whatever it was you said."

The young man raised an eyebrow and looked out the window. He was strangely hesitant, and Mary could see that it was her turn to press him.

"That's what I thought," she laughed.

"What?"

"Acting smug and lecturing me about the meaning of 'things'. But I can see it, you're just as attached as I am. Bet you picked the design of that place because you saw it in some magazine. Maybe that's how you picked your face too. All you ugly little fiends just want to be pretty deep down, after all."

"Don't be ridiculous," he scoffed, seeming to grow more self-conscious by the second, as if even the vaguest accusation that he shared anything in common with Mary were perverse.

"Go on," Mary grinned. "It doesn't matter to you, does it? You'll still have the land. Just burn that monstrosity on top of it, and I'll believe you're serious about your offer. I'll sign the deed, just like you want, and we can call it a night and stop wasting everyone's time. What do you say?"

Now it was his turn to go quiet.

"Unless..." Mary looked out the window. "Your whole scheme was to build a suburb of shitboxes, because you love playing house so much? Maybe that's the problem?"

The man eyed Mary, trying to understand why she was being so insistent, but his expression began to change, his pride and his eagerness to finish things winning out. Before he had uttered a word, she knew that she had him.

The young man looked back out the window and nodded his head.

The flames across the street erupted suddenly, from no single source.

In seconds, the entire concrete and glass house was surrounded by a growing fire. The stone did not burn, but the supports and framing inside began to split and crack as the heat spread.

Mary looked over at her visitor, holding her breath.

He began blinking rapidly, and he touched his throat.

Part of the living room of the concrete house tumbled as a support beam crashed to the ground. Some of the glass at the front of the house began to ooze into liquid, pouring onto the lawn, while furniture inside the structure shrank and collapsed.

"Does it hurt?" she asked. "It's hard to tell with you."

The man opened his mouth to respond, but his voice was only a rasp.

The young man staggered out of the den and toward the front door.

Mary watched from the window as he stumbled across the street toward the flaming house, his silhouette twisting and stretching as the fire raged in front of him.

She imagined that as he stepped across the lawn, he finally noticed, hidden among the blades of grass, the pale, purple vervain flowers, just beginning to bloom—the ones she had planted late at night, well before the foundation in that place had been poured, when she had wandered onto the Abra lot, so small and scattered that they probably never caught his eye before.

She still remembered the sensation of the soil, the dampness of it, as she placed the seeds around the property in the right formation, the beginnings of the traveler's knot that would eventually, quietly bind him to that body and to that home.

The young man now turned to look at Mary in the window. There was no time to return to her house and try to compel her to release the bond of the traveler's knot, and even if he could stop the flames, the house was too far gone, the inside of the structure crumbling, much as the insides of his body likely were. The young man knew, just as Mary did, that it was too late now to avoid what was coming.

His face began to collapse, like desiccated dirt, and his true appearance emerged from what remained of his head. Mary always had trouble seeing the real faces of his kind, but he, like all of them, looked like a shifting pool of ink to her, blurred and shapeless.

After a moment of stillness, he looked away and continued forward into the house, moving through a gap where one of the large floor-to-ceiling windows had melted away. Mary could only guess, but as he went further through the flames, she thought he was trying to hide himself, not wanting to give anyone the satisfaction of seeing what was happening to him in his final moments.

He stood with his back toward Mary as everything came apart around him, his tall shape disappearing in the crackling and roaring that filled the concrete block as the fire stretched to the glowing, night sky.

Mary went to her porch and sat on the top step, covering her mouth and nose with the wet rag on her hand. Other neighbors were at their windows, or on their front steps as sirens drew closer to the bottom of the hill.

As she watched the sky darken, a vast cloud of smoke growing above the neighborhood, a crow with greasy feathers landed on the eaves above her.

"I don't understand," Yellow Eyes said. "You had him in a knot. You could have struck a deal, made him grovel, work for you, even. Why?"

Mary did not turn away from the flames. "Maybe he did something to piss me off."

Yellow Eyes watched the fire, as entranced as everyone else.

"Next time you try to play both sides, you'll remember this, though, won't you?" She looked at him coldly.

The crow turned a solid yellow ring of its eye at the old woman, flexed his wings, then took off toward the top of the hill without another word.

By the time the ambulances and fire trucks arrived, a couple of the house's walls were leaning and another had fallen.

Everything inside had already been consumed.

There was, in Mary's mind, nothing more to save.

In the days after that fire, Mary returned to her daily routine. Standing each morning on her lawn with a cup of coffee, she scanned the dashboards of the parked cars on the street for any without a permit, then she walked down the block to see if any recycling or trash bins were put out early or left too late, in violation of the county code.

When she wasn't watching for unusual cars or strangers entering the neighborhood, she found herself staring at the charred walls of what used to be the concrete house across the street, imagining the old Craftsman in its place while she gripped the Abras' locket in her hand.

Frank would have come slowly down the steps on each of those mornings to retrieve his mail, gripping one of the handrails—sometimes nodding at Mary and sometimes not. But instead, there was nothing but an ugly view of grey rock and blackened wood. Even now, no one was asking where Frank went, Mary realized, and it was unlikely that any of them ever would.

No one ever asks where the old neighbors go, she thought.

Despite herself, Mary continued to dwell on what the young man said to her the night of the fire. As she dusted her sideboards and vases, she often lost interest, like everything had become too tiresome to finish. When she felt that way, Mary wandered upstairs, to one of the quiet rooms that usually sat untouched, the bed inside still perfectly made and flowery wallpaper around it covered with soft light that flowed through sheer curtains.

She knelt in front of a trunk, unlatching and lifting it open, and peered down at a cluttered pile of old dolls and wooden toys, all of them associated with some holiday or birthday that came back to her as she brought her fingers lightly over them.

In those instances, Mary sometimes considered, for a brief moment, finally throwing them out. Her daughter was never going to use them, after all—she would never brew a pot of coffee for Mary downstairs, or chatter away with her in the kitchen while sitting at the breakfast nook, or touch Mary's cheek to wake her up.

Things would never be like they were again, she knew.

But still, she couldn't bring her hands to move, to take anything from the trunk, and she sat paralyzed for longer than she expected. She kept imagining the young man, standing in front of the roaring flames, and thought, for some reason, that she too might begin to crumble and collapse inward, to fall apart bit by bit, if she were to alter anything in the house, no matter how small.

So, instead, Mary put everything back, got on her feet, and then closed the door to the room behind her—each time, more intent than before to leave things in their place, exactly as they were.

See Thomas Ha's story "Where the Old Neighbors Go" online at Metaphorosis.
If you liked it, leave a comment. Authors love that!
Remember to subscribe to our e-mail updates so you'll know when new stories are posted.

About the story

The idea for "Where the Old Neighbors Go" came from my experiences with several different neighbors I had over the years. They were all variations of the archetypal nosy neighbor: aggressive, intrusive, and trying, I think, to make the messiness of the world conform to some kind of imagined order. There was one neighbor in particular who became the genesis for Mary Walker, the protagonist of the story, and whom I got to know much better over several years. While there was nothing I learned about this neighbor that ultimately excused her behavior, I did discover things that I think humanized her and made me understand her perspective, namely, that she harbored a deeply-held belief that if she didn't involve herself in her neighbors' lives (whether putting away their recycling bins or complaining about strange noises), the neighborhood might somehow come undone at the seams.

From there I knew I wanted to write a story where a neighbor like that was actually, unbeknownst to everyone around her, right about that belief: that she was the sole person keeping a threat from tearing the world apart.

By the same token, that threat, a demonic neighbor who moves in across the street from Mary, is based (very loosely) on me and others of my generation like me: young, smug, and indifferent to the disruption our invasion of older neighborhoods cause.

In the end, I found something very satisfying about pitting a character as wily as Mary Walker against an arrogant hipster type and seeing whether, and how, she would prevail.

A question for the author

Q: Do you make art other than prose? What kind, and how is it different?

A: I hesitate to call it art, but over the last few years I've developed an unexpected interest in video editing and digital music composition. My wife is a food writer and cookbook author who occasionally has to create video content for various reasons, so over time I began shooting her videos and composing short music pieces to accompany them. Something about trying to create a visual narrative that makes sense, and editing cuts so that your brain finds a sequence palatable, is a fun challenge that is reminiscent of, but still very different from, breaking out a plot sequence. Similarly, I'm a novice musician, but the thing I've enjoyed most about composing short pieces to go with those videos is trying to evoke a particular atmosphere that enhances whatever it goes with, without drawing too much attention to itself. In that way, it feels a little similar to building themes in short fiction that bolster the story without hitting the reader over the head. Again, these are food videos, so it's not like I'm making a feature film or anything. But what can I say? I get a real kick out of it.

About the author

Thomas Ha is a former attorney turned stay-at-home father who enjoys writing speculative fiction during the rare moments when both of his children happen to be asleep at the same time.

@ThomasHaWrites

Pages Missing From the Diary of Samuel Pepys, Esq.

David Berger

It is well-known that there are several pages missing from Samuel Pepys' famous diary: pages, moreover, that he himself seems to have removed before the various volumes were bound under his direction. Two years ago, the following excerpt was found at Christ's College Library inside a bible that was known to have been owned by Pepys. By a happy coincidence, the discoverer of the pages is Mr. John Rawlinson, a fellow of Cambridge College and a collateral descendant of the Rawlinson mentioned in this excerpt.

Two years have been taken up by exhaustive tests by paper experts, specialists in Pepys' handwriting and in the shorthand code Pepys used for his diary. After all this, the pages have been pronounced genuine!

Because St. Cuthbert's Church, Bedlington, has undergone extensive renovation since the time of Samuel Pepys, no trace of the carving mentioned has survived. There are no known tellings of the story in records of local folklore.

As to the subject matter, it is extremely curious. Pepys, while certainly a collector of anecdotes, some of which were spurious, was never known to be either gullible or to have written any fiction. And these facts lead us to the obvious question: Why were the pages removed? Perhaps we will never know, but a reasonable surmise is that publication of this material might have held Pepys open to a charge of falling for a well-told tale. However, the second portion of the manuscript, dealing with Pepys's own excursion to Bedlington, is even more remarkable.

There are, incidentally, in all the records of the Lost Colony of Roanoke, no records of a family named either Rawlinson or Kent or of a group of Lollard families.

We, the Fellows of Cambridge University, are publishing these missing pages for the first time, and have taken the liberty of naming them the Pepys-Rawlinson Fragment.

29th. In the morning to Westminster-hall to see to some business for my Lord. Afterwards to the house of Wm. Joyce for some coffee, this drink being newly popular in London. It was most excellent and refreshing. Back again to White-hall. At noon my father dined with me upon a good capon with beans and bacon. Afterwards I to Mrs. Alders. She being gone from the house, her maid Miss Clayon and I had a very nice bout, wherein I rattled her up somewhat in her bed. And so home to my own bed.

30th. Up by seven o'clock, and so to work. But before I went out, calling, as I have of late done, for my new boy's copybook, I found that he had not done his work. So I beat him, and then went to fetch my tarred starting rope to beat him further. This article I learned to use for punishments from visits to Navy vessels. But before I got it the boy was fled. I searched the cellars with a lantern. Could not find him. So by water to the Temple, to my cozen Roger; who, I perceive, is a deadly high man in the Parliament against the Court. He shewed me how they have computed that the King hath spended, or at least hath received, about four millions of money since he came in. This is most shocking.

This evening dined at The Crab with a gentleman, a Mr. Coombs, who has business with the Admiralty. Along came his daughter, a perfectly pretty, but quite short and somewhat stout, young lady that lately came up out of the country, particularly Berks. So all by coach to my house, where I found my wife, and we all drank, and then they went away. After, with my wife, to the King's house to see "The Queene at Rest," a new play of Mr. Codgehill, a new playwright. This is a comedy with a goodly part done by that pretty, witty Nel Gwyn. I have never seen such good performing. The Queen and Duchess of York were at the play and seemed to enjoy it with some degree of pleasure. Then we home, and to bed.

31st. Up betimes and at the office all that day, with scarcely a moment to dine. My work being done, that it can ever be done, I walked in the garden of White-h with Captn. Shrewton, where he began to tell me a strange story, which he got on a recent trip to Newcastle. Then there comes into the garden to me Mr. Sleak, that I once knew at Cambridge, and I took him in. Over at the Cheshire Cheese, I called for a surloyne of rost beefe, which we had for dinner. I must note that the Cheese, rebuilt since the Restoration and the Fire, has service as fine as in earlier years. Then we three to the Dolphin, and therewith a quart or two of sacke. Then Captn. Shrewton began us this discourse, which did please us much.

Dining one eve at the Nevyll Inne in Newcastle, a year ago, the Captn. met a prosperous farmer and Justice of the Peace, a Mr. Pepper, who was down in town to deliver a load of hay for the victualling y'rds. And after a shared bottle of Sack, Mr. Pepper told this amazing story, scarce to be believed, but well-known in the country 'round Bedlington, where Mr. Pepper hailed from. Mr. Pepper said these happenings ran their course during the time of his great-grandfather, who delighted in telling this story to whomever would have their ear bent.

According to Mr. Pepper, some eighty years or so before, during the reign of Her Majesty Elizabeth I, a great stone fell from the sky on a farm owned by a Mr. Bowey. The landing of the stone was accompanied by loud claps of thunder and a shaking of the earth around Bedlington. (An account of this stone falling, so says Mr. Pepper, was at one time in the Parish Record for Bedlington.) And when Mr. Bowey and one of his sonnes came out to the fields, they found a great pit in the earth several yards deep. And in the pit was a great hot stone, the size of two large ale butts.

At this time, it being late, after some more ale, and promises to meet next eve to continue this tale, went we home. My wife being still up, I played for her on my flageolette. She did sing finely. And thence to bed.

1st. Early to wait on my Lord. A day of much urgency. The Commissioners of Parliament met this day to make policy over the Fleet. There is some fear of the power of the seamen, who are highly incensed against them because of past wages due. By and by comes in my Lord. We went by water to the Tower. There we dined on a good chine of beef. And he and I did talke of many things in the Navy, one from another, in general, to see how many great things are committed to very ordinary men, as to parts and experience, to do. This doth not please us.

In the evening, to The Dolphin with much anticipation, to hear the story of the events at Bedlington from Mr. Pepper per Captn. Shrewton. We first had a peck of oysters, and then cuts from the tender part of a baron of Scots beef. And after some ale, the Captn. began, to our delight.

So after approaching the pit, Mr. Bowey and his sonne poked the great stone with shovels, and they were amazed. The stone easily broke apart into two halves. And even more dramatick there was within an object very like a brass church bell, but rounded on both ends, like what is called in geometrie a rounded cylinder. This was a thing of beauty and delight. But so hot that Mr. Rawlinson and his sonne could not touch it.

Mr. Bowey spread word by his sonne, and the next day came many townsfolk to stare at the thing. It was agreed by the local folk, by the suggestion of Rev. Rawlinson, the Vicar of St. Cuthbert's in Bedlington, that it should be took over to the churchyard. So, as the stone and the cylinder had cool'd, some local miners made a rigging. The two halves of the stone still warm to the touch was raised.

They was placed on a dray, along with the cylinder, and pulled by four mighty horses to the yard. There the parts of the stone and the cylinder lay until nearly the whole parish was gathered to see this wonder. Even the Bishop came rushing over from Newcastle to see it. And there was talk of perhaps bringing the things, by stages, to London, perhaps by barge.

I remarked that should this have happened in our day, the Royal Society, which I have recently had the honour of being elected to, would have sought this thing out. But the Society had not yet been born at the time.

We then spoke briefly of some of the newest revelations from the Royal Society. Including Robert Hooke's *Book of the Microscope.* None of which seemed pertinent to the business of Mr. Rawlinson's cylinder. I proposed a toast to the Royal Society. Whereupon Captn. Shrewton continued Mr. Pepper's tale.

With the arrival of the Bishop, whose name Mr. Pepper could not recall, the news of the stones and the cylinder was spread even wider. The Bishop sprinkled the cylinder with holy water, and then departed. That evening, the Parish Council decided to employ several miners to break open the cylinder. The effort to begin the next day.

All the next morning, three miners from one of the collieries bashed at the cylinder, that was hanging from a set of blocks. Suddenly, there came a great cracking sound. The watching crowd gave a great exclamation as the cylinder broke open. Mr. Rawlinson led the townspeople in a rousing cheer. Looking inside the lower part of the cylinder, the miners saw a strange box. One of them reached in and brought it out. He having no difficulty lifting it. The box was a gleaming black. And it measured about a yard by eighteen inch, by eighteen inch.

Having listened to this tale, herein shortened considerably, for several hours, and having enlivened ourselves with some good porter, I suddenly began to feel sleepy. And so I gave my excuses to the company and invited them to meet on to-morrow at Ye Olde Cheshire Cheese at Fleet Street. Then Captn. Shrewton and I walked into the City. We parted, he to go to the inne where he is lodging, and I home to Seething Lane and to bed.

2nd. Early with a Mr. Heatherton about Sir Wm. Penn's concerns in reference to Fleet victualing. The details are many and will involve much time. Dined with Mr. H at Mr. Crew's, on my favourite venison pasty. After dinner I went to the Cheese, where I found Captn. Shrewton and Mr. Sleak waiting for me, they having supped. The Cheese held but few people, which I thought strange, wondering if there was some event that night at Court.

And so, after a glass or two of a good sack, Captn. S continued the story of the events at Bedlington. So, said Captn. Shrewton, whose Christian name is Wm., like my Lord, the miners shewed the box, which was of black metal, to the Vicar, Mr. Rawlinson. The box seemed all of one piece. And no way was there to open it. One of the miners suggested that he try to breake open the box with his sledgehammer, but this was objected to by Mr. Bowey. He asserted that the box, being found on his land, was his property. Some words were said about this and some small monies were exchanged. A message was sent out, instead, to reach a certain Thom Woodcoke, from a nearby hamlet, which was a smithe of great skill. It took near an hour to fetch this Woodcoke with his tooles, who came only on a promise of a good payment.

Woodcoke used his smallest hammer and chisel to tap about, just below the rim of the box. And, suddenly, with the tiniest hissing sound, a split appeared, and it became apparent that the box had a lid. Gingerly, Woodcoke lifted the lid, and a great wonder was seen by those standing around him. Inside the box was a Babe! An ordinary Babe, naked, but wrapped in blankets. It appeared to be asleep, but after a moment the Child opened its eyes and gave out a lusty cry.

Mrs. Rawlinson, she the Vicar's wife, took up the little one in its blanket and cooed and cuddled it. Whereupon, the Child reached up and poked at the good woman's nose and broke it! This causing a flow of blood onto her face Mrs. Rawlinson shrieked, and her husband took the Child from her. He held it at arm's length and shook it angrily.

The Babe gave another cry and shrugged the Vicar's hands away with a strong shake of its shoulders. This caused Mr. Rawlinson to let go. But instead of falling to the ground and hurting itself, the Child, wonder of wonders, floated in the middle of the air. It slowly rotated itself around, and flew into the air: first up perhaps thirty feet. And then it flew away to the steps of the church ab't one hundred feet away.

The Vicar and his wife, followed by the parishioners, ran over to where the Babe had come down. Mrs. Rawlinson, goodwife if there ever be such, lifted it up again. The Babe then began first to cry and then to coo. She wrapped it up again in its blanket and held it against her breast. And declared that she would raise the Child as her own. At the time, all could see that around the Babe's neck on a wire was a large and intricate amulet, covering almost half its chest.

There is a carving on the church wall that shows the Child leaping into the air, but some say this is an old carving of an angel in flight. Some say it is a demon.

Afterwards, the great rock was pounded up by the miners and the residuum dumped in a pit. The cylinder was brought into the church, but it was melted down for cannon during the Civil War. And the box and robes of the Babe were kept for many years in St. Cuthbert's. Until one night thieves broke in the Church and stole the box along with a pair of silver candlesticks. (These were candlesticks that the Vicar, not Mr. Rawlinson but one of his successors, had saved from looting by some troopers calling themselves Soldiers of His Majesty but 'twere mere looters.) The thieves had also started a fire to burn down the Church. But it had been put out. But not before the Parish Record and many old documents of the Parish and the Church had been consumed as well as the vestry.

"And that's the end of this tale," said Mr. Captn. Shrewton loudly. He had become red in his face with the ale he had drunk. Mr. Sleak and I questioned him closely about this marvelous event. What color was the great stone? How heavy the cylinder, &c. But the Captn. recalled to us that this was a story he had got from Mr. Pepper, who had got it from his grandsire, who had got it from his father. Who it was by no means clear had been a witness. And anyway it was a tale of Mr. Rawlinson and his wife, not of Mr. Pepper's family. I thought this remark to be a naif one. And one which, with the missing rock, and the cylinder, and the Parish Record also missing, cast a pale light on the tale. This might have been a fanciful story gotten up to explain the carving on the church like many monsters on our old cathedrals from which many olde tales have arisen.

So home by carriage, and I with my head full of thoughts of Mr. Rawlinson's great stone, and the cylinder, the box and the Babe. I ate a bit of bread and cheese. And so to bed.

3rd. Up early but then lay pretty long in bed gaining pleasure with my wife, and then to Westminster, where the Commons is sitting. Here I met with various mediocre folk, who did give me petitions for preferment. Thence to ye Cheshire Cheese, but I found myself not willing to speak to any of my friends there. Having Capn. Shrewton's tale much on my mind. Then to finish my letter for Sir W. Batten, himself Surveyor of the Navy, on errors in the methode of procurement of stores for the Navy and rumors of peculation.

It being three o'clock ere I had done, when I come to Sir W. Batten, he was already in a huffe, which I made light of. To my distress, he found displeasure with my letter. But he signed it, though he would not go to my Lord Chancellor's. So I, myself, presented it to My Lord's Secretary. The rest of the day, at White Hall, I hoped to hear further news about the letter, but nothing, and then home to supper, and they we sat together very lovingly, and then we to bed. Even so, I was much disturbed in my sleepe.

4th. Up early and by carriage to White Hall, and there I worked again my letter criticizing the whole business of Navie procurement. That eve, I came to Sir W. Batten to further discuss the letter, though he now liked the letter well. I down to the Tower Wharf, and there got a sculler, and to White Hall, and so I delivered it to Sir W. Coventry, in the cabinet, where I leave it to its fortune. And I by water home again, and to my chamber, to even my Journall. And then comes Captain Cocke to me, and he and I drink a measure of sack and have a great deal of melancholy discourse of the times, giving all over for gone, though now the Parliament will soon finish the Navy Bill for money. He being gone, I again to my Journall and finished it, and so to supper and to bed.

4th. Up and to the W-Hall and amazed to discover preparation of a coach and four to be put at my disposal. Because of my letter, I am dispatched to Newcastle there to uncover the state of the Navy procurement. It is now being said that peculation and theft have wrecked the condition of foodstuffs and shipbuilding there. At noon to the Three Tuns, where D. Gawden did feast us all with a chine of beef and other good things, and an infinite dish of fowl. Thence to W-H. The coach being ready, it took me home for my kit, whereupon I am off to Newcastle for the inspection. The coach departed from my home at 6 in the evening with the weather being on a sudden set in to be very cold.

7th. Arrived at New Castle this morning at 8. We arrived there just as it commenced to rain hard, and the horses to fail, which was our great care to prevent. Thus ending a cold, hard journey. To sum, nothing but cold and wet and some of the most miserable innes I haf ever slept in. As we proceeded north, the food became worse and the wenches uglier, with the weather. Entering the Yard, the coach brought me to the offices of Sir Donald Dulking, Adm. of the Yard. I then dismissed the coach and instructed the driver to return to L, expecting to journey home by packet boat.

I was soon informed that the Adm. was onboard one of the ships, inspecting a cargo consignment. (Strange actions for an Admiral, I think.) I was exhausted and was urged by the Adm's adjutant to partake of the regular Navy (not Naval officers') mess. I found the provender to be disgusting, but I was assured by my escort, a young Midshipman named Davis, that the Admiral himself regularly partakes of the regular mess. I left the table wholly unsatisfied. A half-bottle of inferior claret did not mollify me.

After a long wait, I finally met with Sir Don'ld Dulking, Rear Adm. We discussed the issue and he agreed there may be some corruption present, but it is of a trivial nature. He invited me to tour the Yard and even board some of the ships, which apparently is his wont. But I preferred to review the accountables. After some hesitation, I made the acquaintance of three of the Yard's bookkeepers, non-Naval men. These three affected a very casual demeanor which, in ordinary, would have offended me greatly. But in their stances, along with the behavior of the Adm., I have become suspicious.

That eve, after finishing the first few hours' work with the bookkeepers, I expected to be formally received by Admiral Dulking or one of his senior staff. But no such event took place, which, again, I took ill. Young Midshipman Davis approached me rather timidly and said that he had been instructed that I was to be housed at the Senior Officer's Quarters. I asked if there were a good inn nearby. And the lad said there was, just outside the Yard gate. It was called the Old Charles. We walked over there just as it began to rain hard. We sat and talked about the Yard. Then there came to us an aged sea captain, a summat foolish man named Captain Seabright. And he and I entered into a great but humourous dispute concerning whether the Navy were better now than during the Protectorate. This discourse took us much time, till it was time to go to bed. but we being merry, we bade the Midshipman goodnight, and continued to drink.

As a stab in the dark, I asked Cap'n Seabright if he had ever heard of Captain Shrewton. He said he had, but had not seen him for several years. I then asked of him if he knew of a Mr. Pepper, a farmer from the vicinitee of Bedlington. To my surprise, he told me that Mr. Pepper is a cozen of his on his mother's side. And he had just come in to New Castle. After a quart or two of wine, the good Cap'n agreed to bring Mr Pepper for breakfast in the morning so I might speak to him, and I to bed.

8th. I had a strange dream and having kicked my night clothes off, I got very cold; and in the morning, and had a good deal of pain. This and the rain made me very melancholy. But when I went down for breakfast, I found Cn Seabright at table with the gentleman Mr. Pepper. This was the manne who first recounted the tale of the Babe to Cn Shrewton (who repeated the tale to me and my friends); he being exactly the manner of stout and rcdd-faced farmer you might think of. The pain that I had got last night by cold had not yet gone, and troubled me at the time. Captain S, Mr. Pepper and I enjoyed a breakfast of a fresh halibut and small beere.

In short, Mr. Pepper confirmed to me the main of the story of the Babe of Bedlington, as he had heard it from his grandsire. There were still, he said, some remnants of the storie, including the pitt when the Greate Stone had been broken up. He told me that he would be returning to Bedlington on the morrow, and if I cared to join him, the journey would be but 16 mile. I could rest over at his farme which, he swore was large and cozy. I agreed and we will depart from this inne tomorrow afternoon, after I hope to have concluded the Navy business here in Newc'le.

So up and to the Navy Yarde and about business. I examined people as to what they could swear concerning the vittles, cordage, Etc., that is being supplied. And I can only, when joined with the worke of the the Acc'ts, conclude that the whole is become the business of cheating rogues and peculating knaves. For part of my examinations, Admiral Dulking sat with me. I conceive that he was uncomfortable as some of the blame for this criminal behavior must fall towards him for which we hope he can give explanation. Thence after the examination, it being too soon to go to dinner, I walked up and down the Yarde, not helping but to notice what I felt to be an overall melancholie.

At last got back to the inne and dined well on another halibut, which was very welle prepared with a mustard sauce. I being cold to my bones, to bed presently, and had a very bad night of it.

9th Sabbath. I slept till 7 o'clock, it raining mighty hard. I know not what will become of the corn harvest this year, as we have had but four fair days this month.

After breakfasting alone on some cold oysters, soup and a half of claret, I was hailed from my table by a voice from the inne y'rd, it being Mr. Pepper. I joined him on his handsome hay cart and greatly enjoyed the trip to Bedlington, as the rain stopped almost as we set out.

Arriving in Bedlington, Mr. Pepper invited me to his home where we sat and talked, and drank, and ate an hour or so. He gave me directions away to the Church of St. Cuthbert's and lent me a horse. He begged me to ride it to Newcastle and leave it at the stables in the Navy Yarde whence he would retrieve it the next week. I replied that I would and parted with Mr. Pepper, resolving to myself that I would do him some preferment when I returned to Newcastle. It took but a half hour to reach the Church, whereupon I searched about for the vicar. And finally, having encountered some ancient natural, I was led to a small building, barely more than a shadde, behind the Church proper.

This lowly place was the vicarage, and to my delight, the current holder of the parsonage, Rev. Mr. Johnson, was at home. He received me cordially and delighted me with a second breakfast. It so turned out that Mr. Johnson is a close friend of my cozen, Angier, at Cambridge and knew, slightly, my brother John. Mr. Johnson being a bachelor, I was introduced to his only housemate, a terrier dog that closely resembles a lamb, but Mr. Johnson assured me, is of both a gentle and powerful nature. I learnt that the reason for his modest way of living was that the former vestry had been burnt by the Protector's men during the Civil War and that it had never been rebuilt. He himself, he declared, was of simple taste and required nothing more although he said the shadde doth need a new roof. This pleased me much, and I resolved upon return to London to speak of this gentleman and perhaps obtain funds for a more adequate home for him. I reminded that the Member of Parliament for Morpeth, Mr. Dowling, is an old associate and I could no doubt catch his ear in this matter.

I begg'd of Mr Johnson if he knew anything of the story of the Childe or Babe of Bedlington. And at that he seemed summat uneasy. I pressed him as far as decency allowed, and, at fin, he took me to see the carving on the wall of the church of which I had heard. This effigy is on the northwest wall of the church. While

Captain Shrewton recounted that it demonstrates the Child in the air, this is not clear. Mr. Johnson said that the image was damaged by the same Soldiers who had stole the box with the Babe's clothes. They had hammered at the statue, hurting it much on grounds it were idolatrous.

Then Mr. Johnson showed me the pit where the residuum from the great rock was put. There was not much to see but a dark set of rock, slightly below the level of the ground. (I took up a small piece to present to the Royal Society.) I then asked the Rev. if he knew anything more of the Babe itself and of the Rawlinson family. He said to me that the subject was so long ago, it was still of great pain to the village and people did not discuss it. I took this as a sign that he would speak no more of this and so I bid him farewell.

I was ready to take my leave of Bedlington. However, after I left the vestry for my horse, the same ancient natural I had seen before accosted me, seizing me by the arm. He asked me, if I wished, if it pleased me, to see something marvelous concerning the Babe of Bedlington as he called the Child. He said he had listen'd at the doorway to the vestry and overheard some of the words I had had with Rev. Johns'n. I did not desire to traffick with this creature, but he importuned me several times. Half speaking, half mumbling. I was almost ready to strike this lout, but his constant talk of the Babe halted me. He signed to me that he wished to drink and pointed to an establishment a few furlongs away. We walked there together, but I bade him walk behind me as his stench was very great. He also carried on his shoulder a sack which seemed quite heavy. I went into the inn and brought out for him a pot of small beere, which he drank in one swallow. He signaled for more, which I brought him. Soon, he talked a great while about my going down with him to Newminster Abbey, which were, he said, six or seven mile from Bedlington. I was anxious to start back to Newcastle and from there back to London, but each time the ancient mentioned the Babe, I felt my stummick stir. And he promised if I went with him, he would shew me something that would astonish me.

So, a certain madness took over me, and we set off for Newminster Abbey, the ancient walking and I riding. He told me his name was Raulph Kent, and he claimed to be near one hundred years old. I doubted this as it would make him much the oldest man in Britain. But I noticed that the beere he had consumed made his discourse more reasonable. I asked him how he came to know the story of the Babe of Bedlington. He said to me that now he and I had left the towne, he would tell me his story. Most remarkably he claimed to be Raulph Rawlinson, the sonne of the Reverend Rawlinson, he who adopted the Babe, which I scarcely believed. And I thought he might be a rogue who was playing a trick on me to get money of me. But I said to him that I thought it wonderful that he had lived so long. I begged him to recount the story of the Babe after his father and mother took the Childe to be their own.

As we proceeded on this short journey, which he promised me would be but an hour but which turned out to be nearer two, this was his story. He had no hesitation nor was he a man of few words. And despite his gruffness and foul appearance, he spoke in a kindly and gentle manner with even some education. He told me that he was only in the towne fortnightly to see Rev. Johnson who gave provisions to him. He had just left the vestry when he first saw me. Then he begun telling me the *Tale of the Babe*, as I have called his story.

As Raulph Rawlinson told me, soon after the Reverend and his wife declared at the churchyard that they would adopt the Babe as their own, within a very few days, they were visited by one Rev. Exton, a dependent of Lord Tankerville. Mr. Exton told them they must either give the Babe up to him or leave the parish forthwith and that he, Rev. Exton, would take over the parish. Raulph's father declared it was his Christian duty to shelter the Babe. And so after all things were ready, with much sadness, his father and mother, he, his sister Elspeth, and the Babe, who they named Willielmus, left the Living of Bedlington and moved to Morpeth where they rented a farm with a dairy herd of Chillingham cattle. Raulph, who was being educated in a school in Bedlington, with hopes of attending university some day, and enter the ministry, saw his education end suddenly.

Life was very hard for the family as their neighbors did shun them and few would buy from them, either milk or cheese. However, they were soon secretly aided by a community of five Lollard families in Morpeth. Eventually, they joined this community, and Rev. Rawlinson became the community's leader. The families soon decided that they would all go to the Roanoke colony due to continued persecution of the Lollards.

It was decided by the Rev. Rawlinson that it would not be possible for them to take the Babe, Willielmus, with them to the New World. The Babe was too well known and 'twould be hard to travel with him.

Raulph said that the Lollards, including his father, decided that if the Babe was on a shippe it would probably mean mutinee. So it was sadly decided that Raulph, who was the oldest son and was twenty years of age, would stay on with the Babe, who was then ten years old. Also, Rev. Rawlinson decided to change the family name to Kent, whence the Rawlinsons had originally come from during the time of King Henry VIII.

Raulph said he felt that the events had weakened his father's and mother's mind, and he still could not countenance what they had done. After they departed with the five Lollard families, in great haste, George had one letter of them from

Barbados. In this letter, which he shewed me, it promised that they would find a way to bring him and Willielmus to Roanoke to join them. And then nothing. He presumed that they had been lost when the inhabitants of the colony had been attacked by the red Indians. After this, the man was quiet for a while.

We finally reached the Abbey, it being very dark in the woods there. We walked thence amongst the great trees that had grown up in the ruins of the Abbey, and in and out of the fallen buildings themselves. And there Raulph Rawlinson finished for me the *Tale of the Babe*. That he being but twenty years of age was left behind with Willielmus, who was but ten but who had the strength of a grown man and more.

And, he could fly like a bird, Raulph whispered to me. So, he told me, when his brother was frightened, he would leap into the air and fly to the top of any tree nearby. I felt amazed by this but I remembered how the Babe had flown from Rev. Rawlinson's hands to the nearby church steps. T'was a moment before I could speak and then I gave out to Raulph Rawlinson to continue.

The farm, he said, did not thrive. Raulph had no gift for dairying and a few years later, he, even with the help of his brother, could no longer sustain the herd and they quit the rental of the animals and the farm. So he and Willielmus became vagabonds, never straying too far from Morpeth and Bedlington. Willielmus's strength let them be able to maintain themselves. In the spring and summer and in the autumn, they worked on the farms. However, in winter without a house, they lived in the Abbey but in a very poor situation, so that they nearly froze or starved.

Towards the end of one colde season, Raulph went alone to Bedlington and begged some food of the new rector, who gave him some of the new vegetable called the potato, which sustained them till the spring. But labour was plentiful and despite Willielmus's strength, they could get no work. One day the two went to Morpeth for the market, perhaps to pick up some work carting, and there was a local faire with a wrestling shew. There was a champion named Wild Bull Boggy. And there were a prize of £1 for any man who could remain in the ring with him for but five minutes. £1 was more than Raulph and Willielmus could earn in a fortnight.

So, Willielmus urged Raulph to let him fight although he was but sixteen. And he, Raulph, was afraid not that his brother would be hurt or even lose, but that with his strength, something would needs happen, and his identity as the Babe would be revealed. But Willielmus, whom Raulph called Willie, wanted much to fight. And so he went to the ring. Wild Bull, Raulph said, was a truly enormous manne, weighing perhaps twenty stone and above six and a half feet tall. Some said he were the tallest manne in Britain.

After some ado, Willielmus climbed into the ring with this gigantic manne. And, Raulph said, his brother beat the other in less than a minute by the glass. But then, came calamity! After Willielmus threw the giant down and the manne could not rise, Willielmus lifted Wild Bull above his head in triumph and shewed him to the crowd. But then, Boggy twisted in Willielmus's arms and punch'd him in the face. And before Willielmus did realize what he did, he smash'd Wild Bull Boggy to the ring, killing him. And then, in great fear, the lad (nought but sixteen, recall) leaped into the air and flew off!

There were, so Raulph described, screams and panick. And someone yelled out that that was the Babe, the Bedlington Babe, grown to be a man. Without waiting to see what would happen, Raulph said that he fled back to the Abbey and hid in a dry well in one of the cellars. He stayed there hidden through the day, all through the night and the next day. Not till the next night did he venture out. Past midnight he heard a crashing sound nearby. Raulph said it is not imaginable how frightened he was as he thought wildly that some from Morpeth were still out for him. But blessed be God, he said, it was Willielmus crashing down from the skye. Then his brother came and spoke to him and said he had been far away in London. That in but a day he had flew from Morpeth to London and back to Morpeth. And Raulph said he could not close his mouth for astonishment and in fear.

Willielmus then said to Raulph that he was determined to fly first to Ireland and then to Iceland, to Greenland and thence to the New World to find their parents. (Raulph added that he had given Willielmus as much education as he could including in geographie.) He had experienced and learnt much flying to London and back. And that he thought he would leave when the sun rose. Raulph told him this was madness. But Willielmus said no, that he must go.

He then spoke to Raulph of the mother's amulet that had been found on him when he was discovered. The amulet, Raulph told me, was about the size of a grown man's hand. Large as it was, Mrs. Rawlinson had insisted that Willielmus wear it round his necke. But when the Babe was but three years of age, to the amazement of all, he had insisted in his baby voice that his mother should wear it always.

Raulph said that once his mother put the amulet on, Willielemus could always sense where she was. And even across the sea, he always had a vague feeling of her whereabouts. And as he was grown older, that feeling had grown. But until he had taken actual flight, he had no notion to seek out their mother and, hopefully, their father and sister.

Willielmus told Raulph that he was determined to go at dawn. Raulph packed some food for him, of what they had. And, true to his word, after much sobbing and embracing and brotherly kissing, Willielmus leaped into the skie and was gone. Raulph never heard from him or the rest of the family.

In the many, many years that passed, Raulph told me he made a life for himself, as before, wandering about and working and living in the Abbey. About ten years after Willielmus flew off, he approached the Rector of St. Cuthbert's, the man who had replaced his father and begged the man for alms. Rev. Exton had become very old, but still hale. He told Raulph that he felt the Church had done poorly with his family. And that he was willing to give him a weekly pittance. And that was continued for several rectors to this day, including the Reverend Johnson. This explained to me why the Reverend had seemed so unwilling to speak to me.

Then Raulph opened an olde wooden boxe and shewed me what he had brought me to see. It seemed nothing but a piece of cloth perhaps an ell squared in size. It were, he said, one of the wrappings that Willielmus was covered in when he were found. And what a piece of cloth it proofed to be! It was of a dull blue and seemed to be some kind of blanket or robe, but small, for a child. Raulph took it up and told me to try to tear it a-pieces. So strong it was, I could not do it. He said it neither burnt nor did it fade or take dirt. I begged him to let me take it back to London to shew to the Royal Society, but he refused, even after I offer'd him a goodly sum. He said he wished to be buried with this cloth as his shroud.

Soon after that, I left Raulph Rawlinson. I gave him a sum of money to help him. And he thanked me. I arrived quickly back in Bedlington, early enough to set out for and reach Newcastle in time for a fine dinner of a capon and some small fish and a bottle of sack. In the morning into London on the mail packet.

12th. At home after a terrible passage, New Castle to London. The weather were foule and I sickened almost as soon as we left the Tyne. And the young cap'n being inexperienced on this run. He brought us perilous close to the Godwin Sands which he laughingly called the Eater of Shippes. Greeted at 6 in the evening at the door by my sweetling, I being more dead than alive. She fed me on some good brothe, which I managed to hold down. She importuned me to tell her some of my journie, which I did. We dined late on some goode beef and claret. And so to bed.

See David Berger's story "Pages Missing From the Diary of Samuel Pepys, Esq." online at Metaphorosis.
If you liked it, leave a comment. Authors love that!
Remember to subscribe to our e-mail updates so you'll know when new stories are posted.

About the story

Somewhere along the way, about a year and a half ago, I got the notion of Superman appearing in the 17th or 18th century. And as a long-time fan of Samuel Pepys, it immediately occurred to me to use his Diary as a framework. (The entire Diary is available online.)

In order to keep Pepys' rhythm, I copied and pasted parts of the book into my story, and then (very freely) converted his words into mine. In the early parts of the book, this was easy because it's mostly a record of his comings and goings and eating and drinking (plus his sex life).

However, Pepys seldom described lengthy incidents, so in the description of the events at Bedlington, and in Pepys' record of his own visit there, I had to wing it. BTW, Bedlington is a real place, and the church is real and the story of the Babe is ... I also did some research about the Roanoke colony and the Lollards to fill in the details.

It was a real trip putting the story together from its various parts. And I want to thank the editors of Metaphorosis for pushing me to lengthen and refine the tale.

A question for the author

Q: What was your favorite children's book?

A: I want to answer this question in two ways: My favorite book when I was a child, and my favorite children's book.

As a kid, my favorite book was *Treasure Island*. After seeing the 1950 movie ("Arrrh!"), I insisted that my Mom get me a copy. She did, and I read it myself in about a week. (I was six.)

My favorite book for kids is *The Once and Future King*. I read it to my own sons.

I believe that the "classic" children's stories and fairy tales have a heft to them that kids like and need.

About the author

David is an old Brooklyn Lefty, living in Manhattan with his wife of 26 years: the finest jazz singer in NYC. He's a father and a grandfather. He's been a caseworker, construction worker, letter carrier, teacher, proofreader and union organizer. David loves life, his wife, and the world. He hopes to help us all escape destruction.

Tower of Mud and Straw I

Yaroslav Barsukov

Prologue

Shea Ashcroft stepped from a carriage into the low-lit cul-de-sac as a mongrel lifted its door knocker of a head from a garbage pile.

Dogs. They'd taken over the capital a week before. The wind dragged garlands of crushed glass and everyday commodities across the pavement, and the dogs picked out anything they could chew: meat from the decimated butcher's shops, greens, someone's shoes.

Those animals had guts. It was the humans who tended to stay indoors—half of them cursing the one person who'd had the chance to 'stop the violence at its inception'. Him.

Three people at the royal court he'd previously considered friends had already advised him to issue an apology. He'd told them to go to hell.

The hound ran to the middle of the street. It barked and leaped in place, snapping its jaws at something it couldn't quite reach.

"Atta boy," Shea said. "Though that bone's a bit too big for you."

The 'bone' hung at the second-story height, the post of a gas lamp stretched like a strut between the opposing buildings, comically, inconceivably. There were reports of looters getting their hands, heaven knew how, on one or two Drakiri devices—*tulips*, his sister used to call them; his sister, when she was still alive— which reduced the weight of anything they touched to that of paper.

Apparently, once you were in possession of something like that, you tried to steal a street light—or had it been a refined vandalism, or a weird attempt at a joke? Shea's gaze grazed the walls for signs of damage.

"Idiots playing with fire," he said to the dog. "If only they risked their own lives alone."

The dog barked and jumped again, heedless of the rubble beneath its feet.

Third door on the right, carved oak. Shea pushed on the doorknob and descended the steps into the basement vestibule.

The valet who took his coat said, "Thank you."

He looked vaguely familiar. Square jaws, eyes sunken into crow's feet.

"Do I know you?"

The man didn't answer, but Shea's memory did.

…the crowd, a huge condensed mass of arms, legs, and throats, rolling toward him, and *back, back, drive them back*, the scent of blood, a lieutenant bending over the balustrade, twisting her body trying to peek into the russet sky—*where's the bloody airship?*—then, the great elongated balloon sailing over the terracotta roof tiles.

Minister, we need your permission to gas the crowd. Snap out of it. Minister. Lord Ashcroft. Shea.

Hands had touched him, shaken him, poked him, but his vision shrank to a girl, pink dress, huge eyes taking in the world as though for the first time, the world in the airship's shadow.

Fall back.

Minister?

Fall back...

The man put his coat on a hanger.

"You were there," Shea said. "In the crowd, next to the girl in pink."

He nodded. "We're all alive because of you, Minister."

But half of the city lies destroyed—also because of me.

He wondered why his title still applied.

Past the inner door was a pocket-size theater, eight or nine rows, six of them empty. Still, a dozen faces—because entertainment had to continue even in times like these, and because, for tiny venues, this was the moment to shine.

All the big ones lay crippled.

Shea lowered himself next to a slender man in black gloves. "Weird place for a meeting. You wanted to see me, my lord?"

"Just Aidan, if you would, my lord. I know we haven't interacted a lot, but I much prefer my own name."

"Why the theater?"

"To make sure we could talk undeterred."

"This week, the street would've sufficed," Shea said.

"Yes, but it isn't safe out there this week. I—"

Applause cut him short. The curtains parted, revealing the scenery: a starry expanse behind something dark and cylindrical. An actor in orange darted onto the stage, doubling up in a bow.

"Queen Daelyn built a tower, took gold from every man, breast milk from every mother..."

So it's about the Owenbeg tower, Shea thought.

He'd seen the official daguerreotypes—a vast column, more of a growth than a human-made structure—but the details were always blurry and the inscriptions read more like statements. 'Biggest building in history'—*try imagining that.*

Shea half-turned to Aidan. "Another play about the tower?"

"The construction effort isn't going well. Something's happened there. People pick up on rumors."

Onstage, the orange man made a leap. "Queen Daelyn sent her servant—to oversee the deed..."

Another, in a silk jacket, appeared from behind the curtain's crimson.

"…the servant wasn't smart enough—and he got promptly killed," the first one declared.

"I heard that rumor, too," said Shea. "That Daelyn is sending someone from the court there. Poor fellow, whoever that will be."

"Actually." Aidan pointed his finger at the silk-jacketed guy. "Actually, that's you out there, Shea. May I call you Shea?"

"What?"

The woman right in front of them turned her head. "Would you please keep your voices down?"

"What do you mean, it's me?" Shea whispered.

"Nothing official yet," Aidan said, "but I was told Daelyn would issue the decree tomorrow. You're to give up your office and become her intendant in Owenbeg. You'll be overseeing the tower's construction."

"What the hell?!" The woman turned again, and Shea said, "Sorry. What the hell, Aidan?"

"I told you—something's happened there, and she needs—"

"I can defend my every action during the riots. And what's an intendant, anyway?"

"The position is relatively new. Honestly, I wouldn't consider this a punishment, rather an opportunity, and that's why I wanted to talk to you—"

He went on, but Shea didn't listen anymore. People onstage jumped, danced, sang in funny voices. Someone behind laughed in irregular intervals. The woman in the front row produced a hand fan.

At some point, he simply stood and made his way out.

"My lord!" Aidan called out, but he continued to the exit.

Outside, the hound had given up on things it couldn't reach and gone back to rummaging through the waste heap.

It seemed like a dream—the slow ride from the city's edge, unloading baggage that all looked the same. Climbing the pier on which the airship perched.

A lady with a southern accent she desperately tried to mask told Shea the first-class suite had been taken, but 'their second class was just as good'. The door she led him to opened into a cabin which resembled a theater prop room, with a couch that stank of sweat, a table, and a vase of flowers overdue for a burial.

"Would you fancy a drink?" the southern lady asked

He said, "I don't really drink."

"Tea, then?"

"Yes, please."

She brought a lone porcelain cup together with a kettle, ice-cold. Shea had no idea if it was another affront or simple negligence—and, frankly, he didn't care anymore.

As the airship slid into a farewell glide over the capital toward where the horizon squeezed the sun of its last drops, he sat and sipped the bland brew. Behind the window, the palace swam by, the Red Hill, the honeycombs of the guard towers' lights. 'Consider this an opportunity,' Aidan had told him.

"I sure hope, Aidan," Shea said now, "that you don't mean suicide."

His sister would've been proud of him, were she still alive: he could've refused the assignment, he could've begged. But there was something noble, romantic even, in accepting an unjust punishment. *There, I made a decision. I would do it again. I bear the consequences.*

If I am to ensure the tower gets built, he thought, *it will be the swiftest and most efficient construction ever.*

And I'll find a way to return, to get back what they've taken from me.

He raised the cup in a mock salute as the palace swam out of view.

There goes my life at the capital, Lenu, sis, my dear thing. After you passed away, I tried to let go, focus on my career—and look how well that came out.

Please forgive that I've stopped speaking to you. I guess the turning point for me was that reception, when someone asked me who you were, at which point I realized I was talking out loud. They thought I was bonkers, and of course it's bonkers conversing with an imaginary dead person—but we're all crazy in some way or another, aren't we? The trick is figuring who's at 'some' and who's already at 'another'.

I wish I had your strength, and I wish you were here now.

I. The Duchy

1

Shea awoke when the ship made a leap toward hell.

Under the daylight's varnish, the cabin took a dive, jolted, plunged. *Maybe we're passing through a pocket of air*, his brain whispered. *Lie still for a minute, it will blow over.*

He tore his hand from the mattress and raised it to his face: the pinky trembled lightly. The next jolt threw him off the couch, and somewhere in the gondola's bowels, two dozen throats produced a collective sigh.

Shea was about to join them when a thought sent him into nervous laughter— *a fall from grace. Perhaps a literal one this time.*

Well, he refused to go out like that.

Still buttoning his shirt, he peeked into the corridor. To his right, the door to the luxury suite swung open, spewing a man in a smoking jacket who sized him up and, in a shrill voice, said, "Are we going to die?"

So, the southern lady didn't lie—first class really was taken.

Shea squeezed himself past the guy. "Don't stand here. Go back to your room and hold on to something."

Behind him, the shrill voice repeated, "Are we going to die?"

"If we are, I'll let you know."

The corridor widened into the dining lounge, pristine white, shards on the floor, cutlery quivering in unison with his own pounding on the bridge door.

"Skipper? What's going on?"

After a good ten seconds, a muffled voice said, "Who is it?"

"Ashcroft." A new dive slapped him against the wall.

The door half-opened, and an acned face appeared in the gap. "Minister?"

"A former one. Let me in."

"Let him in, Jonah," another voice said.

The control cabin was more like a slice of a lighthouse's lantern room than a naval ship's bridge; four would've been a crowd here.

The captain, wearing an olive dress coat of Owenbeg, their destination, stood at the helm—for Shea, he came across as a collection of unconnected details: a wide nape, a sideburn, a crease on the trousers —and the acned face, probably the first mate, clutched a second wheel.

"How may I help you, Minister?" said the captain without turning.

"By telling me what the hell's going on."

"First time in the duchy, I presume?"

"Me and a bunch of other folks, apparently. The passenger cabins are learning to sing opera right now."

"It's just turbulence."

"I know turbulence." The room made another dance move, and Shea grabbed an iron lever to steady himself.

"Please let go of that, Minister," the acne boy said.

"I *know* turbulence. *This* feels like a drunken sailor party."

"A bad day today, that's what it is," the captain said. "It's the air. The air hits *it*, gets pushed in all directions, gains speed. Roughs us up."

"The air hits what?"

"To starboard, Mr. Ashcroft."

Still not turning, the captain waved his hand, and Shea looked. Gasped. Took a few uneven steps toward the windscreen.

Behind it, there was something vast, something dark, a stretch of an evening sky pasted onto midday. To say the tower was colossal was to compare a volcano to a matchstick: it was a mountain's trunk, freed from the foothills, and the scattering of villages in its shadow could've been cardboard toys.

His responsibility? How could he *do* anything to it, *ensure* anything about it?

"Gosh," Shea said, "what altitude are we at?"

"One thousand two hundred feet."

"How high is the damn thing?"

"A thousand, give or take. And I hear they're planning to put another thousand on top of it—but really, I should ask *you* that, no?"

"Pardon?"

"No fools here, Lord Ashcroft."

At that moment, Shea saw himself from the outside: a noble, barging into the bridge, pushing aside a man who'd probably been saving for a year to book a ride in a luxury suite. The tone, the words. *Skipper.*

He stretched out his hand. "I don't think we've been formally introduced, captain."

"Liam Salas. Welcome to the border, Minister."

"I'm not a—"

"I wanted you to know—I'd actually planned to visit your cabin before you so gracefully waltzed in—I'm happy you're here. It's a difficult subject, of course, politically, but my son was among the protesters."

The handshake lasted longer than custom demanded, which was helpful because, otherwise, the next plunge would've sent Shea to the floor.

"I did nothing a normal human being wouldn't have done," he said.

"You would be surprised."

"One's got to suffer from serious empathy issues to use gas on people."

"And yet the queen gave the order, didn't she?"

The mammoth structure outside grew closer, and Shea squinted. "What are those pink spangles? There, and there. What are those dots?"

"Oh, that. That's the *tech*."

"The tech?"

"Drakiri devices."

Shea opened and closed his mouth, and the bridge squeezed around him while memory served up an image of a different room, gray walls, soot stains, chairs with twisted legs, the odor of something unknown, something foreign, and another scent that turned him inside out—of charred flesh. "This is insane. You're using Drakiri technology to build that thing?"

"I'm just steering this airship. But yes, the builders use the tech."

"Why wasn't it in the reports?"

"How should I know? You must ask the duke—or Brielle."

"Brielle?"

"The main engineer."

"Why wasn't it in the reports?" Shea whispered.

Lena, Lena, look at what they've done.

"I have nothing against Drakiri, or refugees in general," the captain said. "Half the duchy still curses the day Daelyn's father granted them a settlement with us, but I think it was about the only thing the old bastard did right."

"Mr. Silas, believe me, I have nothing against Drakiri, either. But this..." Shea drummed his knuckle against the windshield. "How long have you been using the, the tech?"

"Again, you must ask Miss Brielle."

"Who the hell had the bright idea? ... Drakiri stuff is a ticking bomb. I'm talking from experience."

They both looked out the window, in silence, at the approaching giant.

The worst thing is, sis, I don't always remember your face. Sometimes I see you in a dream, and when I wake up, the details dissolve, dissipate into what the daylight brings: the warmth and the glow and the dust. That's what makes me, a grown-ass man, bawl—the fact you're becoming a memory.

They told me it was all part of the 'healing', Lena. Can you believe that?

2

A yellow trail extended from the airship pier in a relatively straight line; not a proper road, more like a track plowed in the field by a huge finger. At the end, four carriages waited.

Shea let the luxury suite guy pick his horse first; the other passengers, in white and brown trousers and dresses, went on foot. Half must've spewed their guts an hour before, and faces wore a shade of pale, but the eyes glowed: *look at it. Look.*

The tower blocked the sun, throwing a mile-long blanket over the fields, the poplars, and the village cowering at the root of the hill on which the caterpillar of the castle slept. Ants cluttered across the tower's vertical body, half of them suspended by threads at such height that Shea had to raise his chin. Construction workers. Some crawled in and out of the spots leaking pink glow.

The thin band at the horizon was the kingdom of Duma, with their perhaps less advanced, but plentiful, aircraft, and his imagination painted a different sky, crimson, ships raining down in fireballs, the tower's artillery barking. No wonder Daelyn had invested so much into the construction—it was her legacy, the most radical defensive structure ever attempted by man.

His head swam.

In a dash of normalcy, a gaunt driver, leaning against the fence in a kind of transfixed state, stared at the people walking past.

"I'm here," Shea said. "They didn't, by any chance, send a welcoming cortege for me?"

The man shifted his eyes to him. "What?"

"Did they send a carriage for me from the castle?"

"If they did, they sure haven't told me."

They looked at each other.

"Well... Could you at least help me fetch my luggage?"

Even when the horse picked up a steady pace, the tower remained immobile, as though forming a whole with the salmon clouds, a painting on an enormous flat canvas.

In the distance, across the fields, a row of yellow lights floated like will-o'-the-wisps.

"I hope I'm not imagining things," Shea said.

"Wives." The driver clicked his tongue. "Fiancées. Lanterns for the foremen at the construction site who're staying for the night."

"Don't they have lanterns inside?"

"It's a tradition."

In the short breath before sunset, the clouds at the horizon seemed to pick up the glow from the procession—and underneath, a new thing stirred in Shea. Perhaps there was a lantern for him, too. Perhaps something waited to happen behind the tower's contours.

He grabbed that lifeline and tried to focus on the sensation. *It's not over. I'm not finished yet.*

At the village's outskirts, a boy and a girl, a pair of brown dashes for knees, ran in circles, slinging dust at each other.

"Look at him," the driver said. "Look at that guy go."

A man pulled an empty two-wheeled cart at the road's opposite side. There was something about him, something unnatural, and a moment later Shea realized what: he was moving too fast, like a marathon runner but without any visible effort. No muscles bulging. He *glided.*

"A Drakiri fellow." The driver spat, without malice, as if paying some weird tribute. "Can pull those things all day. Those aren't real carriages, though."

"Huh?"

"We call them drikshaws. No place for luggage."

"I hate the idea, being carried by another human being," Shea said. "Or a Drakiri, doesn't matter. I can't understand how anyone wouldn't find it offensive."

"Only don't tell 'em that, boss. Will smack you on the head with the whole cart. Strong, those fellows. 'Lot stronger than you and me."

"Yes, I've heard as much. Still, a job doesn't become less degrading because it's easier."

"Few other jobs around here, boss. You can work the fields, but they don't care for that."

Eyes on the road, the Drakiri dashed past them.

"What about the tower?" Shea said. "I bet one of them could replace a couple human builders."

"They don't care for the tower either. Oi!" The driver smacked the horse on the rump. "They don't care for the tower at all."

"Why?"

The man shrugged.

They rode past the houses, blind lattice windows caked with dust, past a butcher with a beer belly and a dirty apron, dragging his feet as though time marched at a slower pace for him, kids tumbling around in the dirt, heaps of raked leaves.

Triangles of the wooden roofs didn't touch the rising moon but hid the tower, and with it went Shea's lifeline: he was at the border, in as deep a province as it got, on someone else's land, without an office, a foreign graft on the local hierarchy. *This intendancy system—had Daelyn created it just to give failures a home?*

In a sense, he was back to when he'd left his family estate eight years ago.

The welcoming cortege waited for him at the castle gates: a gray-haired woman with a hawk nose. In the sunset, the wall behind her could've been made of sand.

"I'm Fiona, the majordomo," she said—but when he extended his hand, didn't change her pose, the sticks of arms crossed over stomach, fingers which would've made a musician proud had they not been mutilated by arthritis.

Shea chuckled. "The next fanfare I get will probably be at my funeral, right?"

She didn't answer—just quietly paid the driver and led Shea through a side door next to the gates, up a set of stairs, down a narrow path between battlements.

Through the embrasures, the last of the day dissolved: molten sun dripped along the tower's edge, a black furnace.

"We're going into the oldest part of the castle, Kayleigh's Wing," Fiona said without turning or lowering her pace. "Kayleigh was the first duke's daughter."

"I must admit I've never been much of a history buff."

"Your quarters will be in that wing. Don't worry, we strive to keep everything in order."

"Thank you."

"The duke expects you in an hour," she said.

"Nice joke."

"Do I seem like a joking type to you, my lord?"

"He wants to see me at, what, ten?"

"At this castle, we work day and night."

"Especially at night, apparently. I've just arrived, and it was a long trip—at the very least I'd need to take a bath…"

"And that's why I said 'in an hour' and not 'right now.' "

Another set of stairs, this time leading downward to an oak door built to survive a battering ram.

The quarters looked posh at a first glance: living room the size of a country house, two couches under green velvet, an exit to a balcony, six gas lamps under the ceiling, all of them working; through an archway, a royal bed and a tapestry depicting a battle at the castle's walls, likely caused by baron A seizing a cartload of sheepskin or something similarly important from baron B. An enamel bathtub, reasonably white.

On closer inspection, the floorboards grunted under Shea's boots, the first wooden wall panel he touched rocked under his fingers, and moths had taken a good bite out of the couches' velvet.

Fiona stood in the doorway, waiting for him to finish his survey.

In the bathroom, he twisted the hot water valve, but only a sound came out, a lone rustle trailing along the castle's intestines.

"Where's the hot water?"

"From nine till eleven in the morning," Fiona said from the entrance. "This isn't the capital, Lord Ashcroft."

It was clear she'd rehearsed the line.

Hence the urgency, Shea thought. Drag out the new guy, tired, sweaty. Let him learn his place. Well, he could play this game, too.

He turned the second valve. The water was ice against his fingers.

"Tell the duke I'll meet him in two hours, my lady. Please send someone to wake me in one."

"The duke has—"

"I don't care. I'll meet him in two hours, or he'll have to find something else to discuss with his people. I heard weather's always a safe choice." He glanced at his own reflection above the sink. "Make sure you rehearse this line, too."

3

The duke didn't receive him in the council chamber or the great hall or any other place normally reserved for official meetings. A servant led Shea back between the battlements and into the 'new castle,' diving into a labyrinth of narrow passages, a succession of U-turns whose main purpose was, most likely, to create an illusion of space.

No, the duke received him in a drawing room, which, of course, sent a message: Shea was a guest here, an important, but ultimately a passing one.

The windows were holes into the night, but the walls reflected warm yellow, as though life had dipped everything between them in amber to wait for Shea's arrival.

It was a scene from a painting: a thin man in his sixties on a satin couch, already wearing a rehearsed sardonic smile on pursed lips; to his right, a group of five: four fellows—looking like someone had fashioned them from the same piece of wood—and one woman. They couldn't have been waiting for him more than ten minutes, but because of the yellow glow and the affected poses, it seemed as though they'd been here forever.

"Welcome to Owenbeg, Ashcroft," said the duke.

"My lord, the queen extends her—"

"Oh yes, how is the old fart Daelyn doing?" The man came alive, re-crossing his legs and leaning on his palm. "Dear all, did you know we had the same teacher of astronomy when we were kids? She was smarter than me, I'll give her that —the only problem is, it's not the stars she was chiefly interested in but the boys'—"

Shea blinked. "My lord, I'm not sure it's appropriate, in the presence of a lady—"

"Yes, yes, let's dispense with the pleasantries. Everyone, this is Shea Ashcroft, *former* Minister of Internal Affairs, *former* councilor to the queen, and, starting with today, an intendant in our humble domain. Whatever the hell that means. As for this lot..." He waved his hand theatrically. "This is Patrick, my military counselor, Cian, Counselor of Justice." He recited the other first names, omitting the titles and surnames. "Miss Brielle is our chief engineer at the tower."

A red-headed woman of thirty–thirty-five stood closest to the couch, perfect oval of an open face, somewhat heavy figure. The men kept their gaze on their master, actors waiting for a cue—she was the only one who looked Shea in the eye. Smiled.

"And this," the duke said, "is Lena, my Counselor of Arts."

For a moment, for Shea, the duke disappeared.

What are the odds?

Not just the name, but something in the profile, the posture...

Standing in the corner, looking out the blind window as though not a part of the reception—which was why he hadn't noticed her before—Lena was half a head above everyone else save for him and the man whom the duke had designated as 'Patrick'. She wore a long dress the color of her hair, a black wave rolling down her back, framing her face with its sculpture-precise features.

He'd never heard of an arts counselor, and, anyway, the duke didn't have a reputation as a patron of arts; most probably, they shared a connection. *Lovers, then*, Shea thought.

"How about a drink?" the duke said.

"I don't really drink, my lord."

"Do I understand it correctly that your primary function as intendant would be sending reports to Daelyn?"

"Not quite, it's—"

"How often?"

"Queen expects monthly communiques."

"Marvelous." A smile. "Marvelous. Let's agree on a day, say, first Monday of the month—Fiona will visit you to provide you with notes on the construction effort."

So that was how he wanted to play it. His majordomo as a censor, pristine reports stripped of all the details Daelyn 'doesn't need to know', omissions legitimized by Shea's own signature.

"Shall we take a step back, my lord?" he said. "Before we agree on any course, I want to fulfill my tourist's duties."

"Meaning?"

"I'd like to visit the tower."

The smile widened, but the duke's eyes were two ponds on a winter day.

And now for the real game.

"Why?" he said.

"I must assess the progress myself."

"We'll provide you with all the details."

"Same as you did with the Drakiri tech?"

Lena, who, until then, had appeared lost in thought, turned her head exactly enough to meet Shea's gaze. They held eye contact for a few seconds, and he continued, "The queen heard you'd met with problems."

The duke's face went red. "Fools' lies, all of them."

"My lord, if I may," the chief engineer said. *Brielle.* "We've used the Drakiri devices to speed up the construction—"

The duke waved her off. "That's what we did. Isn't it what Daelyn wants?"

"I can't speak for the queen, but I have a hunch she wants this venture to succeed, not for the tower to crack like an egg. Which will happen if you keep using the technology." Shea turned to Brielle. "How soon may I visit the site, my lady?"

She opened her mouth, but the duke broke her off again.

"Do you have a background in construction?"

"No."

"Exactly, because you've what, you've led a shoe factory? Before becoming a minister?"

"I've managed an upholstery workshop, my lord. It was a family enterprise. Fairly big, too—we supplied..."

"Big as my ass." The duke slapped the arm of his chair. "I don't care."

He could afford profanity. He had at least twenty years of a head start in politics, and this was his turf.

Everybody in the room stared at Shea, including the tapestry griffins on the wall.

He could press them, push his status as the queen's envoy—but wouldn't that make the situation worse?

"Listen, I understand you feel I'm intruding upon your authority," he said. "I'm only here to help. We want the same thing..."

"There." The duke propelled himself from the couch. "There. You sit at the Red Hill and you think you know what it's like out here. Let me tell you: you don't. For Daelyn, the tower's a vanity project."

"No, it's an anti-airship stronghold. Same for you, same for her."

"All old Daelyn sees is a symbol of pride. We need the bloody thing if we're to survive."

"So it's about survival now. I'm sorry, my lord, but the fact that you border Duma doesn't make it—"

"Oh really?" The duke marched toward Shea, stopping halfway, at the invisible demarcation line where his posse's space ended. "Have you seen their crown prince? The one who's been running the country ever since his father had a stroke?"

"That's pure warmongering and you know it. Even when I was a kid—someone has always been talking about Duma attacking us."

"Go across the border." The duke stabbed a finger at the black window. "I implore you. Visit Poltava. *Their* village, but half the people are *ours*, from before the boundary changed. Or rather, *were* ours. See what they've done to the place, see it for yourself."

"Then there's the question of the sabotage attempts," Patrick, the military counselor, said in a suddenly clear, resolute baritone. "Who but the crown prince…"

The duke, who'd been shifting his weight from one foot to another, froze in mid-motion, and a new expression flickered in his eyes. Fear.

Shea took a step forward. "Sabotage attempts?"

"We don't…" Patrick began.

"Shut up," the duke said. "Just shut your mouth. Can you shut your mouth for me?"

"I'm looking forward to you providing *all the details*," Shea said.

Brielle raised her chin. "My lord, I don't think there's any harm in showing the tower to Lord Ashcroft. Honestly, I don't think there's any harm in showing it to anyone."

The duke gave the paper-white Patrick a long stare. Then he shifted his gaze to Brielle, probably considering whether he should continue the sparring match. "Do it, then," he said and strode out of the drawing room.

Did I win this round, or was I considered too small a fish?

The woman in the black dress turned and crossed the room, too—no, she *glided* through it, sailed-dashed past the befuddled lords whom she didn't grant a single word, disappeared behind the same door the duke had, and left Shea still trying to hold the gaze which wasn't there anymore.

Lena, the duke's lover, was a Drakiri.

What are the odds? To meet someone with your name here, the rarest imported name in the country.

There are other echoes. The way she holds her head, the pride. The eyes.

She probably sleeps with the duke, though, so we won't interact much.

And anyway, Lena, I'll never talk with anyone the way we talked.

4

Morning breathed the coming winter, thin mist that bleached the air, seeped through the embrasures, snaked around the bastions before finally dissolving into sediment on the balcony's floor.

Past the battlements, the tower was over-sized theater scenery showing nothing of yesterday's promise, and the courtyard below him stood empty—as did the balconies to Shea's left and right.

He listened: only a 'caw' came, which could've been someone trying to fix a cart's wheel, but was more likely a crow clearing its throat. *We work day and night*, Fiona had said, yet the old wing didn't simply suffer from drowsiness—it looked dead.

He went out into the corridor, crypt-quiet. With the tip of his boot, Shea pushed the closest door, and, to his surprise, it gave way, sweeping a view of a stripped stone cage with the skeleton of a couch. Second door, the same, but without the furniture. He went faster, knocking on some doors and throwing open the others.

By the time he reached the staircase, he was reasonably sure the only person alive in Kayleigh's Wing was him.

At the same moment he put his foot onto the first step, a sound bled in from above, someone dragging their feet, someone heavy.

"Fiona?" he said and thought, *Unless she's gained a hundred pounds overnight, that's not her.*

After a hesitation, he pressed himself into the wall. In darkness, a huge figure, stubble on its bald head, shuffled by a few inches away, the scent of sweat mixing with something sweet—how Shea imagined a regurgitated honey mass would smell.

The figure submerged into the corridor's shadows, surfacing each time it passed a gas lamp. And each time, Shea's heart doubled its pace, playing drums on his ribcage by the time the stroll came to a stop at his quarters' entrance.

The man pushed the doorknob with sudden gentleness, reminding him of a prize fighter people had taken him to see once, on a diplomatic mission. That one landed his final blows with the same restraint.

You do that when you know how easily you can break things.

Shea glanced at the gray light filtering from the staircase: from here, twenty seconds across the battlements, with good chances, too: he was much lighter than the man they'd sent to his quarters. Ten seconds up the stairs, a twenty-second sprint to the new castle. Half a minute.

He exhaled and tiptoed into the corridor. He would lock the guy in. Being able to snap someone's neck didn't help against locks, and Shea knew how talkative certain people got when kept in confined space.

At the doorstep, he grasped for the key that wasn't there.

"Damn."

The nightstand. He'd left the keys on the nightstand. He threw a last glance at the staircase, now a bleak spot at the end of a tunnel. Counted another ten seconds.

He pushed the door and stepped inside.

In the living room, curtains whispered and caressed the breeze; the bedroom stood deserted, too, but metal glittered at the table near the bed.

He was halfway there when the guy emerged from the bathroom. He looked down, lacing his breeches, the sweet now mixing with the reek of piss. A stupid thought occurred to Shea—*is he here only to relieve himself?*—when the man raised his gaze. Under his brows, two diamonds reflected void, but the hand, as though separate from the body, dashed behind the back to produce a knife half the forearm long.

When he swung, Shea leaned forward, caught the man's wrist, and pulled the three-hundred pounds mass past him. He hoped to twist the arm and dislocate the shoulder, but the man simply stumbled. Shook him off. Did another swing, from the side, blindly, leaving a bloody trail in the right sleeve of Shea's jacket.

Cursing, he dove behind the assailant's back and threw all his weight into a single punch under the ribs.

And while the mountain of fat and muscles was catching its breath, Shea exercised the only option available to him —to run.

Into the corridor, toward the bleak light leaking from the top of the staircase.

The familiar sound of steps came from above.

Of course. It was logical—whoever wanted to kill him, if they weren't completely stupid, would've taken care of the insurance. Two men going into an abandoned wing might've seemed suspicious, but send one in and then the second to finish the job.

"Fuck," Shea said. "Fuck."

Ignoring the pain, he rammed his shoulder into the nearest door—and immediately slammed it shut again, this time, from the inside.

He took a step back, folding his lips as though to whistle, letting the air seep out.

Two sets of footsteps cadenced toward each other, clack, clack against the stone. When they met, there was a moment of silence, followed by something heavy tumbling.

A contralto voice said, "Open the door, Mr. Ashcroft."

He exhaled.

"Please, open the door."

The bald man lay on the floor with his knees to his chest, one hand tucked under his belly as though in a fit of modesty. The stubble glistened, the gas lamp's light wrapping silver around each hair. Next to him stood Lena, same long black dress as the day before, same wave cascading elaborately down the side of her face. *Those fellows will smack you on the head with the whole cart*, Shea remembered.

"Is he dead?"

"I don't think so."

"Thank you, my lady."

"Don't mention it."

He stepped out into the corridor and probed the body with his boot. "This fellow would probably disagree—nothing to mention apart from you saving my life. My lady, please help me get him into this room." It occurred to him—there must've been such brutes in that crowd of protesters, too, craving only blood, destruction... *Oh dear, how can I even think that?* He squeezed his forehead with his fingertips and the soft flesh of his palm. *Those had been people, innocent people.* "I need to question him."

In one fluid motion, Lena knelt and pulled the man's lower jaw. "Look."

"No tongue!"

"Some things you learn from your neighbors. They do it in Duma."

"We should deliver him to the authorities, then."

She cocked her head. "You're funny, you know that? Considering one of those *authorities* sent him to kill you."

"You have any idea who?"

Lena shrugged and, with two fingers, threw back her hair. "Anyone could've. Patrick or someone else from the entourage, out of fear you would take their place. But the most obvious possibility is the duke himself, though he never mentioned anything to me."

"You and the duke..." Shea swallowed the rest of the sentence. *Why had he said that?*

But she didn't answer anyway.

"It seems I'm not going to win any popularity contests around here."

"Thank your queen for putting you into this. I knew one of them would try to kill you right after the reception."

"And you save every stranger that comes by."

"Shouldn't I?" A half-smile opened into weariness—with what? Her life? Her position? People around her? "Yesterday, you were concerned about Brielle using our technology."

"You're concerned, too, am I right? The fellow who drove me here told me no Drakiri would work at the construction site."

"Have you heard of the Mimic Tower?"

"No."

"You may find it useful to read up on Drakiri history. See you around, Mr. Ashcroft."

She strode away, her gait refined, as though belonging to the life he'd left behind, with its gold, embers, halls, dresses; with its evenings on a terrace at the Red Hill overlooking rivers of light.

"See you around," he said to her back.

5

The tower wasn't what he'd expected.

Officially an anti-airship stronghold, Shea had already had a picture in his mind: of a disproportionate artillery dugout. The reality was nothing he'd ever seen before.

Entering it was entering a city—or rather, many cities. A spiral staircase, wide as a market square, snaked around the inner wall, leaving a vast nothingness in the middle, an abyss that sang with wind and made his head spin. This was a world painted by a lover of chiaroscuro, an addict to strong contrasts: shadows lay in pools of ink, and there were blinding patches of daylight—portals in the tower's side the size of a house, ground-to-air cannons' windows into the wild, one for every two or three of the staircase's whirls.

It was next to those openings that people huddled, each portal its own town, each its own compact habitat: lamps, pulleys and carts, flickers of tinder, hammers banging, yells, laughter.

The tower took the length of the world —only it was an alien world, replicating itself over and over as it climbed to a distant, ghostly gap into the clouds. Or did he stare down a well? Shea's head spun again as up and down flip-flopped like axes on a gyroscope.

This, this *cosmos*, his responsibility.

"Don't look up," Brielle said. "At least not for now. You'll get used to it, Shea. Can I call you Shea?"

"Sure," he said, trying to stop himself from retching.

"I'll show you the fifth level today. That's about three hundred feet above ground."

"Gosh."

"It's nothing, little more than a third of the tower's height." A smile, a cocked eyebrow. "Current height, that is."

"We'll go on foot?"

"Oh, no. No." She patted him on the back. "At least not all the way. You'll see."

She's like a kid ready for a ride across the neighborhood, he thought.

Brielle was on the heavier side, and Shea expected her to pant as they ascended—but she navigated the stairs as though she were flying.

A group of people in aprons, rolled up papers under their arms, passed them by. The first 'town' smelled of roasted meat, and a wooden platform extended from the portal into the whitewashed outside, workers sitting on the edge, eating, drinking, talking loudly.

At the third 'town', he wondered if Brielle had taken him on an infinite journey, a pilgrimage that would end with them growing old and having children, but still climbing, still trying to reach some unknown destination.

"Here it is," she said.

A contraption resembling a wooden cage hung at the abyss' shore.

"I have a nagging feeling you want us to ride in this."

"I hope you don't suffer from vertigo."

"No, but I do suffer from this stupid wish to live."

"I'll take good care of you. Oh, a drink might help—those guys back at the…"

"I don't drink. Why not have this thing on the ground level?"

"So that people don't get lazy."

They stepped into the cage, and Brielle jerked a rope loop. From above, a faint echo came: a pulley squealing.

"How high up does this… ehm, lift go?" Shea said.

"All the way to level five. Two hundred feet."

"I think I've just reconsidered."

"Too late." She winked at him as the wood under their boots started rocking and went into a gentle spin.

The swerving continued, every now and then changing direction while the cage crept up the tower. The wind, coming in through the portals, knocked them against the staircase like a patient visitor at the door.

"You can let go," Brielle said.

At first, Shea didn't understand her, but then, as though in an out-of-body dream, shifted his gaze to his left hand: it had one of the wooden bars in a death grip, soft flesh squeezed white.

"Come on!" She laughed, throwing up her arms, and he unclenched his fingers and thought, *How beautiful people can be when they're happy.*

Sabotage attempts, he remembered. Who would want to destroy this, a wonder, a whole world of its own? His future depended on the tower being built, but now that concern faded, allowing something warm, something big to expand inside him.

I could be happy here, too, I simply need to find my way around all the assholes.

Maybe it was the brain releasing a rivulet of euphoria to help the body battle fear, but the same feeling flushed over him as on his ride to the castle, of a new thing about to be born.

"We're sharing it now, aren't we?" he said. Brielle shot a glance at him, and he added, "Don't worry, it's still your baby."

"It's not like that for me." She shook her head. "I'm not as naïve as you might think. I know someone—you, maybe—will eventually take the place away from me. This is simply—my chance in life, to show what I'm capable of." The smile was an abbreviation this time.

At this height, temperature dropped, and the tower started to breathe fresh moss.

"Honesty for honesty, Shea. Why are *you* here? Normally people want to go *to* the Red Hill and not vice versa. Was it by choice?"

"No," he said. "No, I was shown the door."

The lift squeezed through a rectangular hole, rising to the platform where three men stood waiting for them. Two panted next to a wheel hooked to the pulley, and the third one, in an apron, probably a foreman, stepped toward Brielle.

"Chief Engineer."

She leaped onto the platform, and vertigo gripped Shea's chest again: the lift rocked, and there was a band of nothing beyond its edge. He craned his neck and glanced down, into the spiral world.

Then he took a step forward.

Instead of another portal, the tower's wall opposite resembled a huge toothless mouth into which scaffolds and step ladders poked like dental devices.

"The site of the latest sabotage attempt, as requested," Brielle said. "Whoever they were, I have no idea how they smuggled in that much explosive."

Shea raised his palm, blocking the light coming through the hole—and in his mind, he stumbled into a soot-stained room, coughing, yelling something, knees trembling. *Lena, Lena, sister.* What had he yelled back then? Every word was a reconstruction, a logical approximation.

He turned to Brielle. "Truth isn't fully explosive, but it's always flammable. You know who said that?"

"I beg your pardon?"

"Who's examined this place?"

"Patrick's men."

"And they told you it was an explosion?"

"Yes. Why?"

"Because it wasn't."

"It wasn't an—explosion?"

"Look closely."

She said, "I've seen it quite a few times already."

"Look at the edges."

"What about them?"

"See how they're curved inward a bit?"

"I admit it does seem strange, but—"

"Almost as if *something has sucked them in.*"

Traces of happiness gone from her face, she studied—not the hole, Shea. "What do you mean?"

"I mean what I said—it wasn't an explosion. It was an *im*plosion."

"How do you even create one?"

"Show me your Drakiri devices."

"We'll have to backtrack to the nearest portal."

"Lead the way."

She shrugged.

Two circles down the staircase, purple haze of a swamp spilled out in front of the next 'town'; knee-deep, a group of workers circled an egg-shaped thing rising to their waists, forty to fifty inches along the longer side. The Drakiri device shimmered as though dipped in some strange, otherworldly phosphorus.

"Here it is," Brielle said curtly.

Is she nervous—or irritated at me? He cleared his throat. "So you gentlemen are using the stone tulips."

The worker closest to him, a balding man with the eyes of a sad labrador, raised his gaze. "The tulips?"

Shea nodded toward the purple glow.

"It looks nothing like a tulip," Brielle said.

"It does to me."

"We're using the anti-gravity properties to relieve stress in the parts of the structure," Brielle said. "Allows us to build faster."

"Show me how you handle it."

The labrador guy cocked his head. "Well, one rotates the valve to make it hover and pulls the lever to stabilize it if —"

"*One?* One who?"

"In our crew, it's Michael who normally works with the thing. He's currently two levels below, I can—"

"I want to see you do it."

"I—"

"You *have been* trained on how to operate the devices, haven't you?"

Brielle said, "All our crews have received proper instruction."

"It's simply that Michael has a bit more experience," the labrador guy said.

"And what if he's sick? And you can't wait for him, you're on a deadline? I want to see *you* do it."

The man threw a glance at Brielle, and she nodded, slowly, as though underwater. *On the defensive*, Shea thought, *am I threading too close to her turf?*

"That is, if you don't have any objections, my lady," he said.

She simply nodded again.

Fists clenched, muscles arched under the linen shirt, the labrador guy approached Shea as though walking toward an executioner's stump.

He remembered the girl from the crowd, the pink dress, and his heart squeezed—but it had to be done. He needed a test subject.

"Activate it, please."

The other stared at the lever and the valve, visibly unsure.

"Don't be afraid."

"You need to—" Brielle began.

"Let him work."

The man wiped his palms on his trousers, gripped the valve with both hands, flexed his fingers.

Metal creaked, and the tulip sang—a whistle at first, the voice gained force and deeper overtones. Shea frowned, trying to bury the memory of the gray walls, the soot stains, chairs with twisted legs. *Not now, not now, damn it.* The left end of the device lifted off the floor, and, out of the corner of his eye, he saw people taking a step back.

"Everything's fine, continue."

The worker stopped the rotation and grabbed the lever with one hand, the other still locked on the valve, knuckles white with tension.

Drops fell into the purple glow: sweat, but Shea wasn't sure whose.

"I think I've stabilized it," the trembling voice said.

The song evened out, became dull, turned into a hum.

"Isn't it—" Brielle said from somewhere far away.

The device kept touching the floor on one end, a huge pen in an invisible hand.

"Continue."

Thin fingers lay on the valve again: ten degrees, twenty, forty-five.

Full stop. The tulip started shaking.

"What do you do next?" Shea said.

"I don't know."

"It's still on the ground."

"I stabilize it."

"You already did."

"I turn the valve, then." The eyes glanced at him, begging him: *let me go.*

"What are you waiting for?"

The worker flexed his fingers again and spread his feet apart as though trying to balance himself. This time, he went slower: three degrees, two, one.

Metal moaned, and Shea said, "That's enough."

The man dropped his arms, panting like a runner who'd crossed the finishing line. Shea untwisted the valve until it clicked, and the humming died. The tulip relaxed, the hanging end softly hitting the floor.

Trying to hide his own breathing, he turned to the others.

"Ten more degrees, and this thing would've imploded. I guess you've never seen it, which is good—but I can describe it to you. It sucks in everything in a fifty-foot radius. Everything. Wood, metal. Stone walls. People. Itself. Chews things up, leaves behind twisted remains."

He glanced at the labrador guy and saw him, fully saw him this time, the trousers, baggy at the knees, naive eyes, a stubble of red hair. Sweat stains under the armpits, the evidence of the torture Shea had inflicted. *I'm sorry*, he wanted to say, but then thought, *I can say sorry by making it right.* Same as he'd done for the girl in the pink dress.

He turned to Brielle. "You and I need to talk to the duke."

Your voice comes to me more often than your face does—and I've always thought I was a visual type. Sometimes I'm writing a letter and I hear a certain word or a phrase as you would've said it. Sometimes I say them that way myself.

6

He saw Lena again the next morning.

After a stroll through the village, it was like catching a glimpse of a different world: she stood in front of the castle's gates, a sculpture caught in time, gaze somewhere in the distance, hands hidden in a muff.

"My lady," he said, taking the last steps up the hill.

"Mr. Ashcroft." She smiled—not particularly wide, but still a real smile.

"How are you enjoying the cold today?"

"It'll get warmer."

"I went to the tower yesterday, did you know that? And I remembered you'd mentioned—how did you call it? The Mimic?—I wanted to ask you about it."

"The Mimic Tower. Do you really mean it, or is it just your way of making conversation?"

"I really mean it. I want to understand why your people won't work at the construction site."

"Better if I showed you."

"I'm all for it."

"Are you?" She studied him. "Ever been to a Drakiri settlement?"

"Not that I remember."

"I'm going there right now—today's the Equinox. A festival. I guess you could join me if you have time."

Behind Shea, wheels whispered on the gravel.

"There's my carriage, Mr. Ashcroft."

He looked and said, "I know the fellow."

Fifteen miles away from the castle, the settlement was a bright spot among the cookie-cutter villages and hillocks, small flames of kites fluttering third- and fourth-story high. Owenbeg houses were two stories at most, some of them practically grown into the ground; here, even the trees past the town's walls looked taller, greener, crowns sprinkled with warm paper lanterns: moths ready to take off.

Lena got off the carriage and handed the driver the money. "We'll be back in a couple of hours."

"Should I ask him if he would join us for the festival?" Shea said.

"Don't tease people, Mr. Ashcroft."

"I must admit I had another picture in my mind when I heard the word 'settlement'."

The pavement under his feet was clean, flat, as though smoothed by seawater.

She chuckled. "Makeshift tents and bonfires?"

"Something like that. This looks closer to the capital, only without certain elements."

"Which ones?"

"You don't have to lift the hem of your dress."

From the cold autumn sunlight drowning the opposite end of the street, children came running at them, moving with double the speed normal kids would do.

"Sweets, sweets, beautiful lady, do you have sweets?"

"I guess you've forgotten them at home." Shea laughed, trying to keep his balance amidst the incursion of small, strong bodies. "But they're right, you look beautiful."

"Beauty's in the air, Mr. Ashcroft," she said, tousling the hair of the boy closest to her.

And it was in the air, in an eagle circling the dark blue, in the bunting criss-crossed above the market square, in patterns of veins on the arms of the man who handed them jugs of grog.

"How much do we owe you?" Shea asked, but he shook his head.

"They know me here," Lena said.

"So you're some kind of celebrity?"

"Not me. My mother. She was a famous landscape painter."

A couple passed them by, he in a green velvet jacket, she in a wine-red dress, kissing.

"I don't drink, but I'll have a taste in honor of—how do you call it? The Equinox?"

"Yes."

"Do you yourself paint, if I may ask?"

She shrugged. "A bit."

Shea leaned against a pole and took a sip. "Well, at least we invented sugar ahead of you."

"Actually, we have better." Lena said something in Drakiri, and the old man handed Shea a bowl with brown powder.

"Thought so." He took another short sip. "Tastes good, too. What's that contraption?" He pointed with his jug toward the center of the square.

"A roundabout."

"A science thing?"

"You can't be serious. You ride in it. It spins."

"So you need a person on the outside to rotate it for you?"

"I guess you can run around it and then jump on."

Shea studied her. "Let's try it."

"Mr. Ashcroft, it's for kids."

Perhaps it was the alcohol speaking, but he said, "I feel like a kid right now. This is a festival, isn't it? Let's go for it."

"Go for it," the man with the grog said.

For him, they probably *were* two children.

Lena shook her head. "I can't believe I'm doing this."

Simultaneously, they put their jugs on the wooden counter.

It *was* weird, running in a circle in front of a market square full of people, but as soon as he stepped on the roundabout, everything dissipated in the motion. He looked at Lena, her black wave of hair finally untethered, flowing in the air—the world spun and spun, and chickadees sang, and the light, breathing cold and fading yellow, played between the garlands.

When the grog stalls around them came to a standstill, someone cheered, and a few people clapped.

Lena did a neat bow and glanced at Shea. "Thank you."

"For what?"

"For making me feel..." She stepped back onto the pavement, swayed, and he caught her by the elbow. "You're aware I'm only half Drakiri?"

"No."

"Mother fell in love with a count. He died when I was four."

"I'm sorry."

"I hardly knew him."

They crossed the square, navigating through couples and files of happy children, and dove under a clothing line beaded with oranges of paper lanterns.

"Where are we headed now?"

"You said you wanted to learn about the Mimic Tower."

"I did."

The side street ended at a four-story building, plain-looking with its brown walls and hollow eye sockets of windows.

She led him up the stairs into what looked like a regular apartment-house corridor he would've expected to see at the capital.

"Please give me a second."

She knocked on a door: a woman opened with silver hair woven into two waist-long braids. They exchanged a few words in Drakiri, and the woman disappeared again, leaving the door ajar.

"Isn't she going to ask us in?" Shea said.

"Drakiri don't let strangers under their roof."

The woman reappeared with a folio which she quietly handed to Lena.

At the corridor's end, there was a window overlooking the back yard, and

Lena laid the book on the sill. Through the glass, tree branches played with sunlight, sending golden bunnies on wild romps across the backs of her palms.

"Tamara is an archivist—Mother did some restoration work for her in the past. This tome is from two centuries ago, from when our people lived in Pangania."

"I'm sorry," Shea said.

"For what?"

"The genocide."

"Well, we're still alive. And *you* need to unlearn apologizing; won't do you any favors in Owenbeg."

She thumbed through the book until a picture came up, of a plain with a tower rising in the middle of it, going up to the page's top.

Shea said, "Looks familiar."

"It does, doesn't it? We keep meticulous records. The edifice was three hundred feet in diameter, and we managed to reach one thousand one hundred feet in height before—"

She turned the page, and on the next picture, the tower wasn't the only thing anymore.

From a mountain ridge on the far side of the plain, something stretched out, a column of fat ink, a black finger.

"You see," Lena said, "we believe it was two things: the dimensions and the anti-gravity properties of the devices we used in construction."

"What do you mean? What is this? Your people built a second tower?"

"The second tower built itself. Overnight. And then—"

She turned the page again.

"What are those sticks?"

"The picture's scale doesn't allow for much detail, Mr. Ashcroft. But it's people. People burning."

In Shea's mind, the captain's word echoed—*a thousand, give or take, and they're planning to put another thousand on top of it.* Through the window, the backyard was a picture-perfect pastoral: a strip of grass in the tree's shade, a bench the color of autumn leaves, a dog licking the cool off its paw—but this lazy afternoon tranquility somehow lent credence to the drawing in the book, as though the world had willfully taken on a peaceful face to conceal something horrifying.

"Now you know why you won't find any Drakiri at the construction site," Lena said.

"Why did you sell the duke your anti-gravity devices?"

"We didn't *sell* anything." She leaned toward him. "We *gave* them away, all that we had."

"Because he's threatened you—"

"No. Because we don't want to pull drikshaws anymore. We want a ticket into your society."

"What was inside that second tower? Why were the people burning?"

"It's called the Mimic Tower, and it's a door."

"To where?"

"To hell, probably. Metaphorically speaking. See, Mr. Ashcroft, something came in through that door, but we have no idea what exactly. We know that both towers were destroyed; we can only speculate that the chief engineer thought on his feet and detonated ours. There's the death toll. But as far as people go who actually participated in the nightmare... What we don't have are any records of survivors."

7

A wild vine wove its way in from the balcony, hugging the chipped bricks, trying to escape the cold and the light that turned life into a sketch on yellow paper. But wherever the beginning was, the end lay in a palm that promised something more sinister than a long winter sleep.

The duke looked like a patient gardener frozen in mid-motion.

"You wanted to see us, Ashcroft. I heard you had, what, an optimization suggestion?"

This, the shadows, the damp, the table with footprints of mugs on its surface and one leg slightly unstuck, bent at not-quite-a-cripple-yet angle, this was the council chamber. Patrick sat staring at the wall, as did the other guy—Cian?—while Brielle kept thumbing through a finger-thick stack of papers. She hadn't raised her gaze when Shea entered the room.

Lena was absent—*where was she? At the settlement? In her quarters, drawing?* He realized he wanted her to be here.

Shea coughed. "The suggestion, my lord, is to remove all Drakiri tech from the tower."

"Mr. Ashcroft, please..." Brielle finally glanced at him. "I think you're overreacting."

The duke squeezed his fist around the vine's tail, but still didn't move, eyes fixed on the leaves. "So you're done with your *tourist duties*?"

"I am."

"And you apparently think yourself smarter than all of us? You've been here five days, and gotten to the root of all our problems?"

Shea said, "It takes a look from the outside."

"This is laughable, Ashcroft."

"Is it? I've surveyed three different— what you're calling 'sabotage sites.' At all three, the pattern of damage is consistent with what I call an 'implosion.' As opposed to 'explosion.' It also looks similar to what I've seen of other incidents with Drakiri devices."

"Seen during what, your time as a minister?"

"Doesn't matter. Yes. Think about your people, Duke, the workers." In his mind's eye he saw the girl in the pink dress. *I'm like a cart on a track*, he thought, *I've got no choice. The only thing I can do is press forward.* "What will happen is as follows: I will file a report to Daelyn. Maybe she'll believe me straight away and you'll receive your orders with the next courier. Maybe she'll send someone else to verify. Maybe she will pay you a visit herself. And maybe she'll consider replacing a disagreeable lord who's put a project of astronomical cost at risk."

"I respect Lord Ashcroft's opinion," Brielle said, "but the evidence is circumstantial."

"It is not. It's not even a theory. If you ever gamble, my lady, let's play—I bet everything that there were no saboteurs, only your own workers meddling with tools they can't begin to understand."

"Enough." A whoosh of air, and Patrick flattened his palm against the table. "Why are we discussing this? To me, it's clear the saboteurs came from Duma. It is as you've said, my lord, he doesn't have any expertise in—"

The duke swerved on his heels. "Says who, Patrick? Says a man who couldn't perform a simple task?"

Either he thought himself very clever or didn't even care to mask his words. *Okay, it* was *the old bastard who ordered Patrick to kill me.*

"Perhaps someone's due for replacement," the duke said.

The clumsy intervention, however, played in Shea's favor. Brielle's face went red; she looked at Patrick and bit on her lower lip; she probably didn't know about the assassination attempt, but she understood that the duke was furious with his military counselor, which didn't help her case.

And she stepped in.

"My lord. My lord, I've calculations right here. It's perfectly safe—"

The duke shifted his gaze to her. "I only went along with your original proposal because you promised me it would double the construction speed."

"I admit I was a bit too hopeful with—"

"A bit too hopeful, my ass!" He composed himself. "The speed actually went down because we have to install the bloody things, am I right? And now Ashcroft tells me your people can't even handle them. That the tech endangers the construction effort. Is it true?"

"I've calculations..."

"No." The duke leaned on the table and waved his finger in front of Brielle. "No. I don't want your figures. Tell me if there's a *possibility* of him being right."

"I've calculations," she whispered and looked at her hands. "I don't know."

The duke straightened and slapped his hips. "You lot are amazing. Do you realize how it will make me look once *his* report reaches Daelyn?"

Shea saw in the duke's eyes that the matter was being decided. Brielle saw it as well and, with a jerk, stood.

"My lord, without the tech, we wouldn't be able to build as fast, but we can pull a few tricks to achieve the same speed, yes, there are options if we reject the tech, but it will cost us, a lot—and time, yes, so the speed will again go down in the beginning, but then it will go up—I can run the cost calculations as well, or I'll have someone do it, but please consider it will cost much more, and we will have to employ more people, approximately one new worker per each team. Please consider this, please consider the cost, my lord. We can train the workers more in using the tech. I've calculations right here."

By the end of this near-incomprehensible tirade, everybody in the room had their gaze on her. *It's not about the building speed*, Shea thought, *she's worried about something else.*

A nagging feeling visited him, crept up his arms, squeezed his shoulders: that he'd missed something important.

Did I? What did I miss?

But the duke no longer had patience for fine details. Apparently, there was one thing he hated even more than intervention into his affairs: a display of weakness.

"Have the filth removed from my tower and destroy it—I want no ground left for any rumors. File your report, Ashcroft, and don't forget to mention to the old ass Daelyn that we've cleaned our backyard."

Do you remember us looking at starlight, dreaming of the future, thinking up our tomorrow lives? I go back to those moments—objective memory is still there— but I can't summon the feeling. Something has broken in me, I think. Or maybe was broken. Maybe I broke it myself, to steady myself against disappointment. We go to great lengths to avoid pain, Lena, and we lose important things in the process.

Same as I continue to lose you.

8

A soldier awoke him to help him move his things.

The door to his new apartment stood ajar—he pushed it to find himself in much the same room as before, only bigger, with a fat wine cabinet under beveled glass hunkering against the wall and windows overlooking the council tower and a covered gallery leading to it. In the draught, curtains billowed like sails of a brig ready to depart—or enter the harbor.

"Come in, Lord Ashcroft, I've got a housewarming present for you here."

"Brielle?"

She sat on the couch in the room's darkest part, a bottle of wine in hand.

Shea said, "Well, it's an unexpected—"

"Why? Why did you come? Why didn't you just kill yourself when your queen took your office?"

"What?—You're drunk..."

"I am." She saluted him with the bottle, half-full. "What else should I be now? They've taken *your* life away, and you came and did the same to me. But, shh, listen..." She swung forward, legs crossed. "You didn't only fuck *me* up, Ashcroft.

You're finished, too, do you understand? Because your mission here was what, to ensure the tower gets built? 'Project of astronomical cost' and all? Well, forget that now. We're done, we're both finished."

What did I miss? Cold beaded his forehead. "What are you talking about?"

"I made a mistake, okay? I made a mistake in the calculations. With that foundation's diameter, there's no way we'll reach two thousand feet—hell, we won't be able to sustain the current height for more than three months. It will crumble, do you hear me, it will crumble."

"Keep your voice down."

On stiff legs, he strode to the door—the corridor stood empty—and closed it.

"What happened, Brielle?"

"I wanted this job so much." She raised the back of her hand to her mouth. "I was on a deadline from the old bastard, and I didn't double-check the calculations. I made a mistake!"

"Fucking keep your voice down. Please."

"No, I want everyone to know. I'm tired of trying to cover it up. Let them all know! Patrick, Cian, Lena, Fiona, his whole damn posse. Let them know. Brielle, chief engineer, fucked up her calculations!"

The realization started creeping in. "Please, Brielle. Let's talk. Is there something that can be done?"

"There's nothing. He's already ordered the devices to be decommissioned. That's it."

With the door closed, the curtains languished, placid for the first time. *That's it*, the curtains said, *that's it, you've screwed it all up, and now you can forget about the Red Hill, too.*

You've screwed it all up.

'Queen Daelyn sent her servant—
To oversee the deed;
The servant wasn't smart enough,
And he got promptly killed.'

He'd avoided the assassination attempt, narrowly, but the rhyme's penultimate line had the right pitch.

The mongrel dog snapped its jaws in the air.

"I wanted it so badly." Brielle lowered her head. "Never want anything badly, Ashcroft. I thought, maybe—maybe—it would even land me a job at the capital. At the Red Hill."

Shea considered the room, the chipped bricks, the curtains, the bland finger of the council tower outside.

"I know how you feel."

He wandered to the wine cabinet. Opened it. Took out two glasses.

"How about a drink?" he said.

See Yaroslav Barsukov's story "Tower of Mud and Straw I: The Duchy" online at Metaphorosis.
If you liked it, leave a comment. Authors love that!
Remember to subscribe to our e-mail updates so you'll know when new stories are posted.

About the story

I saw the novella in a dream. I was my own hero, banished from the capital to a province which sheltered a magical race. An exile that turned out to be something more.

Another thing was, I wanted to write a story about architects and artisans. I briefly toyed with the idea of an architect main character, but my knowledge in this area is non-existent and my laziness is great. So there you go—we've got Shea who is sent to oversee the construction of the biggest defensive tower in history.

A question for the author

Q: What is your favourite part of writing?

A: Dreaming. Definitely dreaming. Before putting down the first sentence, I see certain scenes in my head, hear music—that's when the genesis happens. Those pictures stay with me throughout the process, I keep seeing them, and the prospect of writing them motivates me when temptation and sleep deprivation come knocking. Getting there across words and pages may sometimes be a chore, but oh boy is the destination worth it.

About the author

After leaving his ball and chain at the workplace, Yaroslav Barsukov goes on to write stories that deal with things he himself, thankfully, doesn't have to deal with. He's a software engineer and a connoisseur of strong alcoholic beverages—but also, surprisingly, a member of SFWA and Codex (how did that happen?). At some point in his life, he's left one former empire only to settle in another.

www.barsukov.com, @Ybarsukov

Copyright

Title information

Metaphorosis September 2020

ISSN: 2573-136X (online)
ISBN: 978-1-64076-177-3 (e-book)
ISBN: 978-1-64076-178-0 (paperback)

Copyright

Publisher

Metaphorosis
a magazine of speculative fiction

Metaphorosis Magazine is an imprint of
Metaphorosis Publishing
Neskowin, OR, USA

www.metaphorosis.com

"Metaphorosis" is a registered trademark.

Discounts available

Substantial discounts are available for educational institutions, including writing workshops. Discounts are also available for quantity purchases. For details, contact Metaphorosis at metaphorosis.com/about

Metaphorosis Publishing

Metaphorosis offers beautifully written science fiction and fantasy. Our imprints include:

Metaphorosis Magazine
Plant Based Press
Verdage

You can also find us:
@MetaphorosisMag, @MetaphorosisRev,
@Metaphorosis
www.facebook.com/metaphorosis

Help keep Metaphorosis running by supporting us at
Patreon.com/metaphorosis

See more about some of our books on the following pages.

Metaphorosis
a magazine of speculative fiction

Metaphorosis is an online speculative fiction magazine dedicated to quality writing. We publish an original story every week, along with author bios, interviews, and notes on story origins.

We also publish monthly print and e-book issues, as well as yearly Best of and Complete anthologies.

Come and see us online at magazine.Metaphorosis.com

Metaphorosis:
Best of 2019

The best science fiction and fantasy stories from *Metaphorosis* magazine's fourth year.

Metaphorosis
2019

All the stories from *Metaphorosis* magazine's fourth year. Fifty-two great SFF stories.

Metaphorosis:
Best of 2018

The best science fiction and fantasy stories from *Metaphorosis* magazine's third year.

Metaphorosis
2018

All the stories from *Metaphorosis* magazine's third year. Fifty-two great SFF stories.

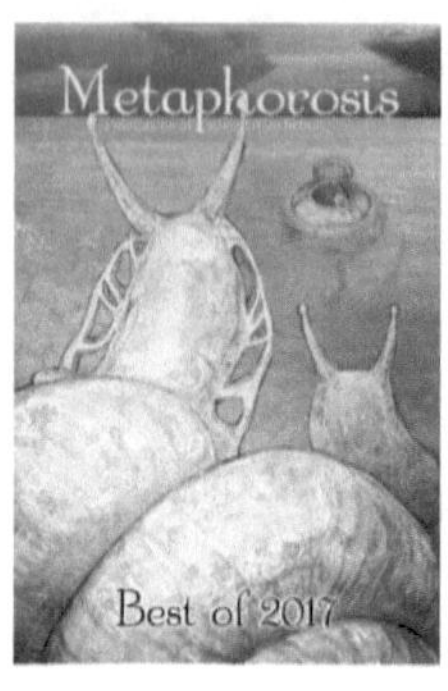

Metaphorosis:
Best of 2017

The best science fiction and fantasy stories from *Metaphorosis* magazine's *second* year.

Metaphorosis
2017

All the stories from *Metaphorosis* magazine's second year. Fifty-three great SFF stories.

Metaphorosis:
Best of 2016

The best science
fiction and fantasy
stories from
Metaphorosis
magazine's first
year.

Metaphorosis
2016

Almost all the
stories from
Metaphorosis
magazine's first
year.

Plant Based Press

plant
based
press

Vegan-friendly science fiction and fantasy, including an annual anthology of the year's best SFF stories.

Best Vegan SFF of 2019

The best vegan-friendly science fiction and fantasy stories of 2019!

Best Vegan SFF of 2018

The best vegan-friendly science fiction and fantasy stories of 2018!

Best Vegan SFF of 2017

The best vegan-friendly science fiction and fantasy stories of 2017!

Best Vegan SFF of 2016

The best vegan-friendly science fiction and fantasy stories of 2016!

Susurrus

A darkly romantic story of magic, love, and suffering.

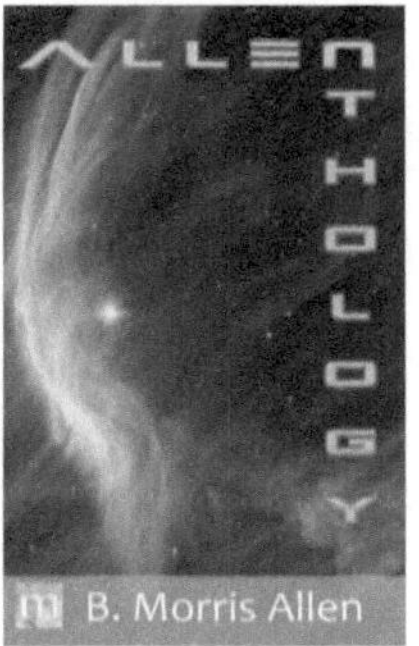

Allenthology: Volume I

A quarter century of SFF, including the full contents of the collections *Tocsin, Start with Stones,* and *Metaphorosis.*

Verdage

Science fiction and fantasy books for writers – full of great stories, often with an additional focus on the craft of speculative fiction writing.

Reading 5X5 x2

Duets

How do authors' voices change when they collaborate?

A round-robin of five talented science fiction and fantasy authors collaborating with each other and writing solo.

Including stories by Evan Marcroft, David Gallay, J. Tynan Burke, L'Erin Ogle, and Douglas Anstruther.

Score

an SFF symphony

What if stories were written like music? *Score* is an anthology of varied stories arranged to follow an emotional score from the heights of joy to the depths of despair – but always with a little hope shining through.

Reading 5X5

Five stories, five times

Twenty-five SFF authors, five base stories, five versions of each – see how different writers take on the same material.

Reading 5X5

Writers' Edition

Two extra stories, the story seed, and authors' notes on writing. Over 100 pages of additional material specifically aimed at writers.

www.ingramcontent.com/pod-product-compliance
Lightning Source LLC
Chambersburg PA
CBHW020330110726
47898CB00003B/822